Stage Call
A Hannah Weybridge Thriller

Anne Coates

RED DOG
UK

Published by RED DOG PRESS 2022

First Edition

Hardback ISBN 978-1-914480-78-2
Paperback ISBN 978-1-914480-76-8
Ebook ISBN 978-1-914480-77-5

www.reddogpress.co.uk

In loving memory of my mother, Joan

ONE

28 September, 1994

"FIVE-MINUTE CALL, Miss Ballantyne." Charlie Steeley, the Assistant Stage Manager, knocked on the dressing room door and lightly touched the letters spelling out the star's name—something he did before every performance, as if some of her magic might transfer to him. He paused, moving from one Nike-clad foot to the other, then continued his usual backstage route, reciting lines from the current play, *Lady Heston Regrets*, under his breath. Sometimes an actor would call out an acknowledgment but more often not, so he wasn't perturbed by the silences. In his mind's eye, he saw the actors staring into their mirrors for pre-performance preparations: facial exercises, voice checks, deep breathing. The image in the mirror became his, the voice his own.

There were only six actors in this play so each had their own dressing room. As there had been a matinée some might have had a snooze between shows. He had been out to buy sandwiches for them from the local deli.

As he neared the rear of the stage, he could hear the animated murmur from the auditorium. A full house. It never failed to excite him. "The smell of the greasepaint, the roar of the crowd…" a cliché, but it was so true. It gave him goose bumps at every curtain call. The exhilaration. The electricity between actors inspired him. He was a part of the magic—even if only in a minor role. *One day*, he thought, *one day*.

He checked the props trolley waiting in the wings, and made sure the whiskey decanter was filled with cold tea. Everything else on set for the opening scene he had sorted straight after curtain down. The minutes ticked by. He ran his fingers through his dark curly hair and took a deep breath to steady his nerves. Nothing would go wrong. He knew that. He could see Coral Moore and Roger Priest standing in the opposite wing ready to come on with their opening lines. For this play, the set was an imposing, Edwardian drawing room. At least imposing from the auditorium. Backstage was another story. The other side of the illusion was far less glamorous.

He noticed one of the armchairs was facing the wrong way. It hadn't been so when he had checked immediately after the matinée. Too late now—the curtain was rising. The audience stilled in delicious anticipation. Coral delivered her opening line, "Darling I really don't know why you had to invite those ghastly Hestons. You know I can't stand her, and as for that dreadful husband…" and, as though it had been a stage direction, Roger, moved deftly across the stage to turn the armchair. There was a puff of smoke, which evaporated with an agonising slowness. Charlie stared in mute horror; into the silence a scream echoed as the chair revealed the strangely still body of their star, Joan Ballantyne.

"Curtains. Lower the fucking curtains," screamed the director into his radio link.

For what seemed like an eternity nothing happened. Then the curtains fell and the safety curtain was lowered; The Old Vic stage was shielded. Away from prying eyes, their extinguished star rested, but not in peace. The house lights came up as all hell broke loose…

THE DIRECTOR, Sir David Powys, had checked for a pulse, which was non-existent, though the body was still warm. He shouted for Charlie to call the emergency services while he made an announcement from the front of the stage: "Ladies and gentlemen, I am sorry to say that this evening's performance of *Lady Heston Regrets* will not be able to continue. Our star, Joan Ballantyne…" he couldn't continue. Should he say she had died or was indisposed? He avoided the issue. "Please be assured that everyone will be booked in for another performance or be reimbursed for their tickets. Thank you for your forbearance."

There was no point in detaining the audience although many, it seemed, were determined to hang around eager to know what had happened. Management took their details. Still some lingered.

The director went backstage and greeted the two uniformed police officers who were first to arrive. They secured the scene.

Backstage, cast and crew reacted in different ways. Coral sobbed into Roger's shoulder. Roger's face was ashen. Charlie just stared, his whole body shaking. He couldn't believe what he had witnessed.

It seemed as though the uniformed officers—and anyone else who dared express an opinion—thought it looked like a clear case of suicide. Except perhaps to the female officer who appeared mesmerised by the dead actress's feet. A detective sergeant soon joined them and organised everyone into units. The director's anguished fury was matched only by the sobs of a make-up girl. Everyone else seemed to have been shocked into silence.

The body of Joan Ballantyne, in full costume, remained on stage. Slumped in the armchair. The glass of whatever she had been drinking balanced precariously in her lap. A hand hovered near the glass, while her other arm hung limply. Her face bore an expression of surprise, as though she had not expected to find herself thus exposed. The golden, elaborately styled wig she had been wearing for her part as Lady Heston had slipped sideways revealing a hairnet that made her look vulnerable and old. Her deep red lipstick looked like blood, smearing away from her mouth. The pathologist moved round her body, taking photographs and dictating into a small machine.

"How long d'you think she's been there?" the DS asked, avoiding the word dead.

"Not that long by her body temperature."

"Any idea of cause of death?"

The pathologist rolled his eyes before answering curtly, "I'll know more when I've done the PM, obviously, but there are no outward signs of violence or a struggle. Could be natural causes or she took her own life."

Overhearing this, Charlie shook his head. The Joan Ballantyne he knew would never take her own life and she'd not shown any signs of illness during the matinée. If anything she looked healthier than he'd seen her in ages. Positively aglow with health and happiness. He thought Joan had looked delighted with herself. He looked around at the people gathered in the stalls and was surprised at their number. He watched the new guy talking animatedly to someone he couldn't quite see to identify. The skin on the back of his neck tingled. He wanted more than anything to go home, but it looked as though they all had to stay until they had been questioned by the police, who were using some of the backstage rooms for interviews. He waited his turn; he had nothing to fear but fear itself.

TWO

HANNAH SHOOK HER head more in acknowledgement that she wasn't up to the task at hand than anything else. She wasn't cut out to collaborate on narrative non-fiction, but that was what she had been commissioned to do by Hallstone Books. It was Lord Gyles' solution for her to keep her mind active and to earn money without putting herself at risk. They had all had a shock at the attempt on her life by Edward Peters at Heathrow Airport. Although he was now dead—having taken his own life—there could be others who were out for revenge.

"A time to take stock and think about the future," is how Lord Gyles had put it. She could see the sense in this and, from what the proprietor of *The News* intimated, she was still or could be a target for people she'd upset with her previous investigations as well. The thought of unknown forces working against her made her feel weak then indignant.

"What do you think?" she'd asked Claudia Turner, when the DI visited after her return from recuperating at her parents' home in France.

"Might be an idea to keep a low profile for a while," Turner had said, as she refilled their glasses. "Mike Benton would be relieved."

"How is the doughty sergeant?" Hannah smiled as she remembered just how many times he'd saved her from a bad situation. Although the last time at Heathrow had been touch and go.

Claudia sipped her wine. "Preparing to leave us for his new job as a Detective Inspector."

Hannah had heard about his promotion. "You'll miss him." Claudia nodded. "He's changed so much since I first met him."

"Not really. He was going through a bad patch. Now he's back with his wife, he's returned to how he used to be. Mike's one of the reasons I'm here. We'll be throwing a leaving party for him and I know he'd love it if you came along."

Hannah made a face.

"He still feels bad about …"

"Well he shouldn't." Hannah's terse reply surprised Claudia. Mike had been standing right next to her on the concourse in Heathrow Airport when Edward Peters, suspected of killing the Australian men trying to find their British families, had stabbed her. The DS had blamed himself, but no one could have foreseen Peters' actions.

"I know. But please say you'll come—you're almost one of the team."

Hannah smiled, and this time her response was genuine. "As if. But yes, I would like to say goodbye properly. Thank you."

Claudia poured the rest of the wine into their glasses. "Any news from Tom?"

Hannah took a large gulp before she replied. "An email now and again. He seems to be enjoying working with the Aussies and loves the lifestyle out there."

Claudia's expression was unreadable. "Good for him. How do you feel about it?"

"Exhausted, if I'm honest. I haven't got the energy for a long-distance relationship. Or any relationship at all, if truth be told."

"Why, have you had other offers?" Claudia laughed at her expression. "I would have thought that doctor—James isn't it?—would have made a move by now."

"James?" Hannah almost spat her wine. "Where on earth did you get that idea?"

"I'm a detective." She laughed. "Then there's his handsome neighbour, Army Mark. I'm sure he has you in his sights. No pun intended."

Hannah could feel the slight flush on her cheeks as she remembered her last conversation with Mark before he returned to his next tour of duty in Bosnia. He had invited her to dinner on his return.

"I see I've hit home there."

Hannah looked even more embarrassed. "I'm teasing you." Claudia finished her drink. "I'd better call a cab."

A SLIGHT DISCOMFORT brought Hannah back to the present. The scar where she had been stabbed had healed nicely, although it still itched from time to time. It had become an imaginary wound. Like an imaginary friend, she thought. However, her nightmares were real. She still woke in the middle of the night, gripped by panic if not pain. She wondered if Edward Peters had intended to kill her or just use her as a distraction. They would never know now. He had killed himself before he was interrogated. When she'd got back from France, she'd gone to see Lucy Peters who had lost both her brother and the son she hadn't known, but she hadn't been at home. Lucy's neighbour, Edith, hadn't seen her for some time, and it wouldn't have surprised Hannah if she'd returned to rough sleeping with her mates in the Bull Ring, a few minutes away.

It would have been better for Lucy if Hannah had never discovered her secret about a son she had produced with her twin brother, Harry. But maybe he would have found her eventually anyway… He had certainly set out to find—and kill—Harry. She wondered if Edward would have reacted differently if he'd known that Harry was not in fact his brother but was both his uncle and his father? Imponderables.

Edith had invited her in for a coffee, and then presented her with a parcel wrapped in brown paper. Hannah looked at her questioningly, only to be met with a smile and a command to "Open it."

Inside was a framed set of what looked like studio shots of Hannah's daughter, Elizabeth. They were fabulous. "How on earth…?"

"While you were in hospital, I met your nanny Janet, and she agreed to let me photograph Elizabeth for you. There's another unframed set for your parents. It's a welcome home present and a thank you."

"Thank you?"

"Your newspaper bought a lot of my photos to go with the massive coverage they gave your story. And they paid me very handsomely."

Her smile was lost on Hannah who was concentrating on the images of her daughter. When she looked up, there were tears in her eyes. "These are beautiful. Thank you so much."

Hannah left shortly after, both women promising to keep in touch.

THE HOUSE WAS depressingly silent around her. Elizabeth had started attending the local nursery. Hannah missed Janet, but was pleased that her former nanny had found a way back into the career she loved as a police officer. Janet had been able to return to her work, as her disabled mother had decided to live with her sister in Essex. Janet was apparently still furious with her mother for what she saw as her treachery in the way she'd led Hannah on during her investigation of the children who went missing after the second world war. Hannah had managed to forgive her own mother. Audrey had been attentive and almost loving when they'd stayed in France. On a walk in the nearby woods one afternoon, her mother had paused by a small pond. She stared into its depths. "When I thought we'd lost you... when I thought you might die... well I couldn't forgive myself for how I'd been... how cold. When you were born, I was frightened of loving you too much." Tears ran down her face.

"Mum please don't..."

"I do love you Hannah. I'm just not good at showing it."

They had clung to each other as a bird Hannah couldn't identify sang out from his perch above and, laughing, they had walked home arm in arm. Hannah had returned to London with a lighter heart. She had to accept her mother for who she was, not what she wasn't. She couldn't change her mother, but her feelings towards her had improved with the visit. Her father had given her a huge hug as he'd left her and Elizabeth at the airport. "Thank you." His eyes told her everything she needed to know.

Hannah was grateful that when her shifts allowed, Janet often came over to join her and Elizabeth for a meal. Her stomach rumbled, reminding her she hadn't had lunch. She went downstairs to make a sandwich and was just sitting down to eat it while she read the newspaper, when the phone rang.

She was tempted to let it go through to answerphone but picked it up.

It was the editor from Hallstone Books. "Hi Hannah have you heard the news? Joan Ballantyne is dead."

THREE

HANNAH READ THROUGH what she had written with increasing dismay. Rory had contacted her to ask for some copy for *The News's* obituary for Joan Ballantyne, as she had been working on the actress's biography at the time of her death. Not her normal line of work and she wasn't sure about the protocols.

She glanced at her notebook where she had jotted down the basic facts: Joan Ballantyne, actress, was born in London 7 June 1925. In 1950, she married Sidney Hawkins. They had one son, Leo. Marriage dissolved 1970. Sidney died in 1973, the year after she married Patrick James (no children) who died 1982. Joan Ballantyne died London 28 September 1994. As Hannah read, her words seemed hackneyed, but maybe one of the subs could knock it into better shape. She hoped so. Ordinarily she hated having her work edited, but this would be an exception.

"One of our best-loved national treasures tragically died yesterday, on stage doing the job she adored. Joan Ballantyne has many claims to fame, not least for being the first actress to play the sex siren, Helen Dewton, in one of the century's best plays, William Trenton's *No Place to Call Home*, on Broadway in 1957 and most recently for her scene-stealing, Oscar-winning performance in *My Sister's Best Friend* in1989. To win such an accolade for Best Supporting Actress at the age of 64 was, she was quoted as saying, 'proof that you don't need to young and pretty to succeed. But you do need to be offered a fabulous role'.

"Not being blessed with the traditional good looks and glamour Hollywood equates with box-office hits, Miss Ballantyne had played mainly supporting roles in movies: but those in charge of making them pursued her in her later years, especially after her Oscar. However it was always to her first love, the stage, that she returned. And it was on the stage of her beloved Old Vic Theatre that she died, playing the title role in *Lady Heston Regrets*. She once said in an interview, 'I repeat my destiny each time I am on stage. It is there that I am most alive,' which makes her death on stage all the more poignant.

"Joan was born in London in 1925, trained at the Vera Green Academy, and made her stage debut at the age of eighteen in *The Manderson Girls*; she did a stint at Birmingham rep and made her first London appearance in 1945, in *The Rumour*, and her New York début in *The Matriarch* in 1949.

"Returning to London, she realised her ambition to play Viola on stage at The Old Vic in 1950. Following her marriage to Sidney Hawkins in 1950 and the subsequent birth of their son two years later, Joan remained out of the limelight with only occasional forays to Broadway and to the movie studios, making films which have long since faded from memory. But in the seventies, the high points of her British career were her excursions into Shakespeare. She was quoted as saying: 'Nothing can beat the Bard for drama, romance and pertinence to any age.'

"More recently her fan base had extended when she played the part of a grandmother in the award-winning soap, *Chicory Road*. She was only scheduled for a few episodes, visiting her family, but was such a hit that the producers kept her on, only to write her out of the series in a street accident which killed several of the cast. Fans were bereft. But television's loss had been theatre's gain. Until Miss Ballantyne's mysterious death on stage.

"Joan is survived by her son Leo Hawkins, granddaughters Olivia and Freya, who live with their mother in the US and her younger sister, Eileen."

Hannah sighed and looked over the quotes she had been sent. "I have lost my best friend and the world will be a poorer place without her," wrote actress and friend Diana Stowbridge. Sentiments echoed by her agent Caroline Maston: "Joan Ballantyne was a star in my agency's firmament. She was a loyal and compassionate friend who will be missed by all who had the privilege to know her." The director of *Lady Heston Regrets* wrote, "I am devastated by Joan's untimely death. She was an absolute joy to work with and her loss to the world of theatre is immense."

Maybe that would do. *The News*'s showbiz writers would probably add their own thoughts about Joan. She hoped so.

FOUR

"BUT WHY WOULD my mother have been shopping that morning and bought a fridge full of food, and ordered a book at Waterstones, if she intended to kill herself that evening?"

Hannah studied the furious face of Leo Hawkins. The actor son of Joan Ballantyne was even better looking in the flesh than he was in his celebrated television roles—the latest of which was a new crime series in which he played a forensic scientist. His slight tan was accentuated by a crisp white shirt. His hair looked tousled as though he'd not long come out of the shower, and his hands clenched and unclenched rhythmically. He stood up suddenly and strode across the room to peer out of the window of his fifth floor Kensington apartment.

Hannah had been caught off-guard by Leo's phone call the day before, when he'd invited her to meet him. The request was more of a subtle command—a man used to getting his own way. A man who had people clamouring to please him. For all that, he had actually sounded relieved when she had agreed. And now he stood stiffly, dressed casually in jeans and a white shirt, open at the neck, as though his grief were gripped within his slim body. Torturing him.

Hannah took the opportunity to look around the room. There was a grand piano in one corner, which housed a cluster of what looked like family photos. She knew Leo Hawkins was divorced and had two daughters aged nine and seven. She wondered how often he saw them and how absence had affected his relationship with them. Joan had told her that she missed seeing the girls growing up but her ex-daughter-in-law did send her photos and made an annual visit from the US.

She had expected to see photos of the glamorous and famous but apart from a few modern art prints and what appeared to be an original, signed L. S. Lowry, the walls bore no witness to his acting life save for a large portrait of Joan Ballantyne, which looked as though it had been taken relatively recently. There was a look of the coquette in her eyes—whoever the photographer was, he had created a beautiful vision quite at odds with the woman Hannah had been working with. The interviews for her biography were often sprinkled with barbed comments about co-stars, directors and— most vitriolic—theatre critics. However, Hannah had to admit that in the short time she had known Joan Ballantyne, she had never seen her depressed or in low spirits. She had too much fire in her.

Leo turned back to face her, hands thrust in his pockets, his expression a curious mix of grief and bewilderment. "I can't bear to think of her dying on her own, like that. She must have been so scared, Hannah." There was nothing she could say to reassure him so she remained silent.

"One always imagines sitting by a parent's bedside, holding hands and making your final farewells." He made a visible effort to control his emotions. "None of this makes sense. My mother was definitely not depressed. She had a joie de vivre second to none and she had no money worries or health concerns. It just doesn't add up. I spoke to her that morning. She was calm—well as calm as she ever was— scathing about one of her co-actors, and happily making plans for when the production went on tour."

Playing devil's advocate, Hannah said, "Perhaps your mother was unhappy and hadn't liked to worry you?" She remembered reading somewhere that the decision to end their life can make that person seem happy. Relieved.

He looked at her angrily. "And this… this so called suicide doesn't worry me, I suppose?" He flopped down onto the chair. "I'm sorry Hannah. It's not that I won't believe my mother took her own life. It's that I'm convinced someone killed her and I want you to find out why."

FIVE

AS HANNAH WAS going to be nearby, she had arranged to call in to see Lady Celia Rayman and Mary. She felt a pang of guilt at how long it had been since she had visited them and she was looking forward to catching up with their news. Their house was within walking distance, and Hannah enjoyed the autumnal sun on her face as she strolled along the street and considered what Leo Hawkins had told her. His mother, it seemed, had received some anonymous correspondence, which implied the sender knew something from her past and was blackmailing her. What if they had killed her? That didn't make any sense. Why would a blackmailer cut off the source of income?

"But what if—" Leo had stopped pacing and come to an abrupt stop in front of her. "What if my mother had refused to pay up and was happy for the person to go to the press, but someone else was not. Someone who would also have been implicated?"

"Do you know of anyone?"

He shook his head. "That's what I want you to find out. You have access to all my mother's papers and diaries…"

"No I don't."

"Don't what?"

"I don't have access to them. A have the floppy disks that contain her drafts, but your mother kept a tight control on what I was allowed to see. And since her death…" Hannah saw Leo's expression harden.

"I'll rectify that with my lawyer, Hannah."

As she was leaving, he clasped her hand in what seemed an urgent appeal. "You will help me, won't you? I want my mother's killer found and brought to justice."

HANNAH CLIMBED THE steps to Lady Celia Rayman's imposing front door and rang the bell. Mary answered, as though she'd been hovering in anticipation, and enclosed Hannah in a hug. "Lovely to see you, but what a shame you couldn't have brought little Elizabeth with you."

Hannah smiled, aware that she was never the main attraction if there was a chance of her daughter being there. "She's at nursery now and I was on a work interview." She stood back and considered Mary. "You look as though you've lost a bit of weight. How are you?"

"I am absolutely fine and even better for seeing you. Celia is in the drawing room." They walked in together. The room brought back so many memories. Not least the discovery of Liz's bequest to her daughter and the revelation of Lady Celia and Mary's relationship. Those had been such dark days. Today, however, the room was full of sunshine, casting an ethereal light upon Liz's portrait, which hung above the mantelpiece.

Celia, ever elegant, strode across the room and took Hannah's hands in hers. "So good to see you, my dear. But dreadful news about Joan Ballantyne."

Hannah's face must have revealed her confusion. She hadn't told them who she was visiting or why.

Celia answered her unspoken question. "I saw the obituary you wrote in *The News*."

Hannah smiled. "Not your usual reading matter, surely?"

"It has been ever since…" the 'ever since' hovered momentarily like a rain cloud between them. Ever since Hannah had exposed the people—or some of them—behind the murder of their daughter and her best friend, Liz. "And, of course, Lord Gyles has become a friend."

Of course. He was probably involved in the trust Celia and Mary had established in their daughter's name. His association with charities was, Hannah assumed, a way of ingratiating himself with those who were not so impressed with the exploits of his publishing empire.

"We were so glad to hear he had you working on Joan's memoir."

Mary put an arm around her. "Keeping you out of harm's way."

The way Celia had pronounced "Joan" made Hannah suspect they knew her more intimately than through her obituary, but she was prevented from asking more by Mary handing her a glass of sherry. "You have this with Celia, while I put the finishing touches to lunch."

Hannah knew it was no use saying she couldn't stay. They so obviously enjoyed having her here and she had been remiss in her friendship. She raised her glass to Liz's mother and sat down in the armchair opposite her.

"How are you both?"

"We're fine and keep ourselves busy with the trust and our charitable interests. But before Mary gets back, let me tell you something about Joan."

Hannah's curiosity was piqued.

"We met at the Vera Green Academy."

Hannah nearly choked on her sherry. "You went to drama school?" This was an unexpected revelation. Liz had never talked much about her parents' lives, but she thought this would have warranted a mention.

Celia gave her an arch look and continued. "For a while, we were close friends. Then I married, and she went on to become one of our national treasures." Hannah could almost see Celia describing the quotation marks in the air and smiled.

"So I suppose you lost touch."

"We did. Well apart from Christmas cards and the occasional phone call. But when our children were young, we did see more of each other and she contacted me when Liz died. In fact she was at the funeral."

"Was she?" Hannah had very little recollection of Liz's funeral at St John's at Waterloo—the same church where Liz had run her dentist's clinic for the homeless in the crypt.

"Yes, well she didn't stay long—I think she left when we went off to the crematorium—but I had a long letter of condolence from her. Remembering our times together. I think she always knew about Mary but never spoke of her suspicion. She was such a private person herself. Which was why I was surprised that she was sanctioning and helping with a biography."

Hannah had finished her sherry and placed the glass on the table beside her. "I think it was to try to stop other people writing about her. She had control over the content and the book was 'the authorised' version of her life."

Just then Mary came in. "Lunch is ready. We thought we'd eat in the conservatory to make the most of the sunshine while we still have it, Hannah."

SIX

GOING HOME IN a cab, Hannah felt pleasantly relaxed from lunch. As usual the food had been delicious and lovingly prepared, always accompanied by Mary's home-baked bread and a deliciously crisp white wine. Images floated in her mind. Celia as a drama student. Joan as another young mother comparing childrearing, and then it hit her and she was totally alert. Celia mentioned another baby. Or rather she'd mentioned another pregnancy. Yet from all her research, Joan Ballantyne had only ever had one child. Her son Leo Hawkins. She took out her notebook and wrote a memo to herself to check that out. It might be nothing at all, but Celia was rarely wrong in her recollections.

Celia and Mary had been remarkably circumspect during lunch. No, Hannah corrected herself, not remarkably. They never asked intrusive questions, or pried into her personal life. But Mary did ask, "And what about Tom, my dear, is he still away?"

Hannah paused to consider her reply. She didn't want to seem needy or a wimp. "Yes he's still in Australia. I think he rather enjoys the lifestyle there and, of course there are a lot of loose ends to tie up. Although that's all very hush-hush."

"Of course." Celia topped up their glasses. "Well, don't be a stranger. We have missed seeing little Elizabeth. Are you free for Sunday lunch? Next weekend?"

"That would be perfect. Thank you."

Celia and Mary smiled at each other and Hannah couldn't help but think there was some sort of ulterior motive. But if there was it could only be an innocent pleasure, she thought.

As she was leaving, Celia hugged her tightly. "You will be careful, won't you? When we thought you… when you were injured, we felt so helpless. We couldn't bear to lose you as well."

Hannah noticed the tears in the older woman's eyes. "I promise. I've no intention of putting myself at risk. The last time was a wake-up call." She could still remember thinking she was going to die and leave Elizabeth an orphan as Edward Peters' dagger plunged into her and she lost consciousness.

AS THE TAXI pulled up outside her house, Hannah checked her watch. Time enough to check her emails and any voice messages before she collected Elizabeth from nursery. She looked across the road to number nine, thinking about her neighbours. Leah and her husband had returned from visiting her newly found brother in Australia full of plans and projects. Leah had started a charity helping Australians who may have been victims of the Child Migration Scheme or their children to trace their English families. For a moment she envied Leah her joy and dedication. Then shook herself. She had Elizabeth.

"Miss Weybridge."

Hannah paused as she was unlocking the front door and turned round. A camera flashed, blinding her for the moment. Then she saw who had called her name. A woman of about her own age with a recording device held out in front of her. "Miss Weybridge. Do you have any comment about Joan Ballantyne's death?"

Hannah glared. "No, why should I?"

The other woman smiled in a not altogether unfriendly way. "Well, you are writing her biography and I heard you've been to visit her son, Leo Hawkins."

Hannah could feel the anger welling up inside her. "For heaven's sake, have some respect for the dead."

"Pot, kettle, black, I think applies here."

Hannah was about to reply then remembered the tape recorder. Whatever she said could make matters worse. So she finished unlocking the door and went inside. The woman called after her; Hannah didn't hear the words but felt an incipient threat. How did she know about her meeting today? Even news about the biography had been strictly embargoed.

She dashed upstairs to her study and switched on her computer, then saw there were three messages on her answerphone.

"Hannah I've just been door-stepped by some hack. Just wanted to warn you in case they turn up at your address." Leo Hawkins' voice sounded weary.

The following message was from someone who didn't identify himself: "Ms Weybridge I read your piece in *The News*—not very well researched if I may say. There are things I could tell you about Joan Ballantyne, which would make you think differently about her. I'll call again."

The last was a familiar voice. "Hi Hannah, please call as soon as you receive this message. Rory."

HANNAH'S HANDS WERE shaking as she dialled Rory's number. He answered on the second ring, as though he had been waiting for her call, but then said, "Hi Hannah, could you hold a moment?"

She could hear voices in the background. One of which was the editor's. Georgina Henderson didn't sound happy and Hannah was glad she wasn't the unknown recipient of the dressing down.

"Sorry about that Hannah. It's mayhem here at the moment. I just wanted to warn you that someone has leaked some info about the Joan Ballantyne biography you're working on and..."

Hannah interrupted him. "There was a hack on my doorstep when I got back home and I've had a message from Leo Hawkins to say he's been doorstepped too."

Rory was quiet for a moment. She wondered if the mention of Joan Ballantyne's son had instigated it, but couldn't think why. It was on the cards she could have met him when she was interviewing Joan.

"Okay. Listen could you come into the office? We'll send a car. There's going to be a meeting—more like a post mortem—in an hour. George is furious and Lord Gyles is going to honour us with his presence."

It was the last thing Hannah wanted or needed. "It's rather short notice. I'll have to organise a babysitter for Elizabeth and..."

"Bring her with you if you can't find someone."

Hannah had never heard him so abrupt. "Okay send the car." She hung up and rang Janet's mobile. She had given her the phone as a leaving present. A rather cheeky gift as it meant Hannah could reach her at any time. "I don't suppose you're free now are you?"

"On my way home. What's the problem?"

"I have to go to a meeting and I need Elizabeth to be collected from nursery and looked after until I get back." Hannah's breathing calmed knowing Janet was available.

"That's fine. Don't worry, I still know where everything is and I'd love to spend some time with Elizabeth. Just let the nursery know."

"You are a godsend. Thank you so much. I'll ring you later to let you know what time I should be back."

Hannah went down to the kitchen and drank a couple of glasses of water. Back upstairs, she refreshed her makeup and hair and collected a warmer jacket. The evening air would be much cooler later. She was ready by the time the car arrived and tooted. Carefully locking up, she gave silent thanks that Janet had agreed to keep her keys and be on standby for babysitting. Thank goodness she had been on an early shift today. As she walked to the car, she didn't notice the man who watched her intently from across the street while he spoke into a radio, then walked off in the opposite direction.

SEVEN

HANNAH HADN'T BEEN to *The News* offices since just before her last exposé about the Australian men killed by Edward Peters had hit the headlines. His attack on her at the airport had made her a major part of the story. Rory and his team had taken over the writing while she was in hospital.

On her return from recuperating at her parents' house in the Loire, she had been grateful to Lord Gyles, who had recommended her to his publishing house to assist Joan Ballantyne with her autobiography. It was a secret project, as they didn't want another publisher to rush out a spoiler. Joan Ballantyne was an intensely private woman, an actress who valued her reputation for being an enigma. She had just lost her role in *Chicory Road* when she'd agreed to play the part of Lady Heston at The Old Vic. Her exceptional performance received universal critical acclaim, which seemed to bring her personal life into sharper focus.

To Hannah, she seemed self-absorbed with more than a little of the prima donna about her. However Joan Ballantyne could be charming when she wanted to be and the commission meant Hannah had work, which would pay the bills and keep her out of harm's way. Now it seemed to be a poisoned chalice.

The car pulled up outside the offices and Hannah paused to take a breath before getting out. The last time she'd been here there had been a car bomb incident and an attempt to abduct her only stopped by Lord Gyles' timely arrival on the scene.

"You getting out miss or just admiring the scenery?"

Hannah's face flushed. "I'm sorry, I hadn't realised you were in a hurry." Her sarcasm was lost on the driver.

He stared back at her in the rear view mirror and she could feel the hairs on the nape of her neck tingling. Maybe she was just being paranoid. "I don't need your name to report your insolence." She got out of the car and slammed the door.

Inside the building she was surprised to be met by Rory who gave her a quick hug then directed her to the executives' lift. "The meeting's in the boardroom."

Once the doors on the lift closed, he looked at her. "How are you? You look well." He smiled. "Don't look so worried. Lord Gyles decided we needed to take extra precautions with this meeting."

Hannah was about to answer, but the doors opened into the boardroom where Lord Gyles, Georgina Henderson and the company lawyer, Larry Jefferson, were already assembled. "Come and sit here Hannah. Would you like some coffee?"

"Yes, thank you."

While that was placed in front of her, Lord Gyles looked at her with an expression she couldn't fathom. "This meeting," the lawyer said, "is being minuted by me and is in the strictest confidence." Everyone nodded.

Hannah swallowed hard to try to dispel the bitter taste of fear in her mouth.

"It seems we have a mole," Lord Gyles said without preamble. "Someone has leaked the story of the Joan Ballantyne autobiography. Now it could be that that someone has added two and two seeing your obituary, Hannah. But I think it goes deeper than that." He looked across at Georgina.

"After the last fiasco we had with the security men, I think there is someone deeply embedded in our company." Georgina spoke quietly and Rory nodded in agreement.

Hannah looked around at the concerned faces that all seemed to be looking at her. "You surely don't think..?"

The legal eagle coughed. "How secure is your home Hannah?"

Hannah laughed. "Like Fort Knox. Plus I have someone come in regularly to sweep for listening devices and taps on my phone."

"And what about your mobile?"

Hannah looked at him blankly.

"Is that secure? Does anyone leave messages on it?"

"Sometimes. Not often."

"And your landline answerphone?"

"Obviously a lot more leave messages on that but…"

"We think someone may have been monitoring your calls. That's how they knew about your meeting with Leo Hawkins."

"And how do you know about that meeting?" Hannah could feel her colour rising. Had they been monitoring her calls as well?

"I'm sorry Hannah. We had a tip-off and—" Rory didn't get to finish his sentence.

"And you decided to invade my privacy like that. How dare you?" She stood up and picked up her bag.

"Sit down, Hannah." Lord Gyles' voice was calm, but he spoke with a quiet authority that brooked no dissent. "It wasn't us eavesdropping. But we were alerted to what was happening. Unfortunately so were our competitors."

Hannah sat down. It seemed she would never be free. At that moment the prospect of moving to Australia to be with Tom seemed far more appealing.

"George—" only Lord Gyles could get away with calling the editor that to her face. "You have something for Hannah."

Georgina reached under the table to retrieve a box and pushed it across to Hannah. It was a mobile phone. "This is the latest technology and we've had some specialists programme it for you. Use it for any calls that apply to *The News* or the book company. In fact use it for all your calls. We have this number for you now. That is only the people in this room. We've had a redirect placed on your old number and your landline so people can still get hold of you. You'll need to set a four-digit password to access any messages and each password only lasts for one week." She looked up and smiled at Hannah. "It's for your own protection as much as anything else."

Hannah could feel her scar itching. Her protection? Were there still people out there determined to silence her? Or perhaps they just wanted to discredit her. Either way the thought made her feel sick.

"So what do you want me to do?"

Georgina's smile looked genuine. "Nothing. Just carry on as before."

"The book, of course, will still go ahead. Joan Ballantyne in her own words—type of thing, but you'll get full credit as author. You'll need to have copies of everything stored safely. And be vigilant. I don't think you'll have any more problems from the gutter press."

Hannah almost choked on a laugh. Pot, kettle, black—her mind echoed the words of the journalist outside her house. Still, we all like to think we're better than we are. "Great. But who is the mole?" Hannah looked from one to another of the people around the table.

"We're working on that one." The lawyer smiled. "Just be careful and trust no one."

Hannah sighed. She had thought this book commission was taking her away from all this cloak and dagger activity. Mercifully they hadn't asked why she'd visited Leo Hawkins. Perhaps they already knew. That thought sent a shudder down her spine.

"Did Leo have any new lights to shine on his mother, by the way?" Lord Giles asked breaking into her thoughts.

"He said he'd had some papers that might be relevant."

"Good." They all waited. Her cue to depart.

RORY ACCOMPANIED HER in the lift. "So how are you feeling?"

Hannah stared at the man she had come to regard as a friend. At least, someone who always had her back covered. He had been kind and supportive. She assumed Rory was not suspected of being the mole as he was in the meeting. She wondered why he was. "Trust no one," Larry had said. Did that include Rory? Did she have to be circumspect with him?

"I'm not sure really. Tired. Cranky. Undecided."

"Undecided about what?" His face showed concern, but how well did she know him really? How well do you know anyone?

"Life. The universe. Everything really."

"Isn't the answer 42?"

Hannah smiled. "Nice try. Sorry, but life seems an uphill struggle."

"Would being with Tom help?"

"I don't know. Right now, Australia *does* seem appealing." She laughed, but there was no humour in her expression.

"But I'd miss you."

Hannah thought he was about to say more, but they had reached the ground floor and the doors opened before she could reply.

"There's a car waiting for you outside. Take care Hannah. And keep in touch." He kissed her cheek and she noticed he watched until her car was out of sight.

EIGHT

IN THE CAR going home—fortunately with a different driver—Hannah rang Janet. She had to look up the number as she was using her new phone.

"I'm on my way back. Do you fancy a takeaway?"

"Sounds great. Elizabeth is bathed and ready for bed. I'll keep her up until you get here."

The relief Hannah felt that Janet was there and would stay on for a while was overwhelming. She really didn't want to be alone with her thoughts. She called Dulwich Tandoori and placed her order so she could collect en route home.

Her new phone rang. It was Georgina. "We've spoken to Leo Hawkins and he is happy for all his mother's documents and papers to be sent to your home some time on Monday. He'll pack them himself and arrange delivery through us."

"Thanks. Rather unusual for you to get involved in Lord Gyles' publishing venture isn't it?"

"It's a question of trust, Hannah. If you do have any more trouble on the doorstep, contact me immediately. We want you to recuperate, not be harassed by..." she didn't finish the sentence but rang off abruptly.

HANNAH HANDED THE takeaway bags to Janet so she could sweep Elizabeth up into her arms.

"Mama," her daughter screeched. She looked tired and turned to Janet, "Night, night."

"Night, night, sweetheart. See you again soon."

Hannah inhaled her daughter's pure fragrance as she carried her upstairs and gripped her more tightly than necessary. Elizabeth's eyes were already closing as she listened to her favourite story and soon her regular breathing told Hannah her daughter was asleep.

BACK IN THE kitchen, Janet had put the meal in the oven to keep warm and had opened a bottle of wine. "You looked as though you could do with this."

Hannah sank into a chair and accepted the glass. "Thank you so much for stepping in like this, Janet. I can't tell you how much I appreciate it."

"It's not a problem and you know I love spending time with Elizabeth. And you, of course," she added, seeing Hannah's expression.

"How's the job going?" Hannah noticed a new confidence in her ex-nanny. No, it wasn't new, but it was different.

"Brilliant. I'm so happy—not that I wasn't…"

"I know, you really don't have to explain. I loved having you as a nanny but I know you're back where you belong." She sipped her wine. "Can I pick your brains?"

"Depends what you're after." She smiled and placed the curry containers on the kitchen table.

As they helped themselves, Hannah asked, "Did you hear anything about the death of Joan Ballantyne at The Old Vic?"

Janet paused. "I was there."

Hannah stared at her. "What in the audience?"

Janet snorted. "No I was one of the first attenders. We picked up the call and were nearby."

Hannah looked embarrassed. "Please don't say any more. I don't want to compromise you."

"Nothing much to say. Obviously the cast and crew were distraught and it was chaotic for a while… Must have been dreadful for the actors actually on stage."

Hannah ate thoughtfully. "Yes. It must have been. You didn't notice anything strange…"

"What about an elderly actress dead on stage?" She didn't wait for an answer. "Come to think of it there was something odd. I did mention it to the DS, but he was totally dismissive."

Hannah waited, not daring to prod her in case she clammed up.

"Her shoes were on the wrong feet. Like someone had shoved them on hastily… As though someone had helped her set the scene and was maybe in a rush."

"You don't think she was helped to die then?"

Janet considered for a moment. "At the time, I thought someone had added them as an afterthought. Like not wanting to see your heroine without her shoes on."

Hannah pulled a face. "Bit odd. Maybe it was someone with a foot fetish."

They both laughed. "This curry's delicious." And with that, the subject of Joan Ballantyne was dismissed.

NINE

THE BOXES ARRIVED by Securicor on Monday morning. Leo Hawkins, or maybe Georgina, had taken the precaution of sending the three boxes by separate drivers one hour apart. Hannah wondered what could be in there that warranted such extreme measures, but if what Leo thought was true, the clue to who murdered Joan Ballantyne—if indeed she was murdered—could be contained within.

They'd had a long chat on the phone earlier in the morning. "I'm so sorry, Hannah. I feel that by inviting you here, I inadvertently exposed you to whoever turned up on your doorstep. Did you see Saturday's *Record?*"

She had. She had bought all the newspapers over the weekend, searching out any references to Joan's death. The photograph of herself made her look guilty even though she wasn't. The other photo on the front page was of Leo at his door looking furious. The juxtaposition of the two images made them look like co-conspirators. Or lovers denying an illicit affair.

The headline was scurrilous: *Joan Ballantyne dead on stage but who is comforting her son?*

"I'm sorry Leo, the problem is my previous investigations have upset a lot of people who still seem determined to discredit me. I appear to have led them to your door."

There was a pause. Then Leo chuckled. "Let them think what they like then. I know you are working on the book, but I would like you to look into her death for me. The two needn't be mutually exclusive."

Hannah paused. Her scar tingled. "You're right but I'm not sure how much I can help you?"

"We'll see but at least you have all my mother's papers to work on. You might find some leads there."

"That's true. And Leo—" She paused, not sure about asking him the question uppermost in her mind.

"Yes?"

"This is a bit delicate. Do you know of anyone—a man—who has an axe to grind with your mother?"

"I imagine there must be quite a few. Fellow actors, theatre critics, directors she'd upset. Anything in particular make you ask that?"

Hannah thought back to the answerphone message left anonymously. "Yes. Someone left a message saying my obituary of your mother didn't expose her… her nastier side I suppose."

"How utterly despicable. Who was it?"

"He didn't leave a name."

"Well that says it all. Not much we can do about that. Now on a more cheerful note, I was thinking if the tabloids are going to link us—romantically, shall we say—let's use that against them. Let me take you to dinner—we can discuss this further and give them a run for their money."

Hannah laughed. "That would be fun."

"Right let me know when's good for you. Sometime after you've managed to go through some of my mother's papers? And Hannah—?"

"Yes. Would you mind coming to the funeral? It's on Thursday at St Paul's, Covent Garden."

"That's quick, isn't it?"

"Yes. My ex-wife and daughters flew over as soon as she heard about my mother and they need to get back to the States. To be honest, I want to get this part of it done and dusted. The post mortem has been carried out, so there's no need to wait. And from your point of view, everyone from the show will be there and it may give you some insights. The wake afterwards is at The Old Vic."

She wanted to say no. She'd had enough of funerals. But he was right. It would be a simple way of meeting the last people who saw Joan without making it look like an investigation. Plus *The News* might like some inside coverage.

"Okay. I could be representing the paper. That will be one in the eye for our paparazzi." Something tugged at her memory. "By the way, did you find out what was in the glass your mother was drinking from?"

"Yes the police said it was a mixture of alcohol—a Bloody Mary for God's sake—and pentobarbitone." Hannah was silent. "My mother would never drink before a performance—far too much of a pro."

"But if it was suicide...?"

"It wasn't. She definitely didn't take her own life. Acting was everything to her. She would never have wanted to be remembered in that way. Such a cruel end to her career."

HER NEXT CALL went easier than expected. Georgina seemed to be anticipating her suggestion. "Yes, go ahead. You wrote her obituary, so it wouldn't seem that strange if you attend her funeral, especially as you have been linked to her son."

"But I..."

"I'm teasing you!" Hannah had thought that teasing was beyond the editor. "You could do with taking a photographer."

Hannah was one step ahead of her. "I've thought of that—could you pay Edith Holland the usual freelance rates?"

"Lucy Peters' neighbour?" She sounded unsure.

"Yes you used some of her photos in the Harry Peters case." She managed to make it sound like something that was totally unconnected to her. "She's unobtrusive and—"

"Not a description I would choose—she's rather obvious with her hair and dress sense."

"Then she'll fit in perfectly with the theatrical crowd."

Georgina seemed to be weighing up her decision. "Okay. You've convinced me. When is it by the way? We'll have another photographer with the pack as a decoy."

EDITH SOUNDED AMAZED when Hannah rang to ask her about attending Joan's funeral. "Wow that's brilliant Hannah. Are you sure?"

"I am and so is the editor. It's Thursday at St Paul's Church in Covent Garden. Followed by a wake at the theatre."

"Bit grim isn't it—the scene of her death?"

"Not my call. But it will be good to see you again Edith. Have you seen anything of Lucy?"

"No not for ages. I think she's spending a lot of time at the Bull Ring. Maybe she'll move back when the colder weather sets in."

"Perhaps." Hannah felt guilty that she hadn't been to see Lucy, but she didn't want to remind the poor woman of what her son had done. The memory was too raw for both of them.

HANNAH HAD ALREADY cleared her desk over the weekend and had removed everything from her pin board. That was going to help with the timeline and notes that may need to be included in the book.

The first box contained diaries. Years of them. Hannah was going to have to go through them and cross-reference with other papers and the cuttings the newspaper had already sent her. Fortunately the librarian there had them all in date order.

The second box, which arrived as planned an hour later, was full of photograph albums. These too had been sorted in date order.

Hannah was beginning to think her job was going to be easier than she had thought until the last box arrived. She opened it to discover files and papers, letters and notes—all the miscellaneous paraphernalia of Joan Ballantyne's personal and public life. It was a mess. And it was the obvious place to start.

Three hours later, her back ached from bending over and her hands felt tacky. Time for a late lunch. She was washing her hands when her new mobile phone rang. Only three people had that number—then she remembered that all her calls were being redirected to it. Including those to her landline. It seemed an extreme measure but in the lawyer's opinion a necessary precaution. It simplified matters. None of her calls—business or private—could be intercepted.

"Hi Hannah. Just to remind you about Mike's leaving do tomorrow evening."

It had completely slipped her mind. "Right. What time and where?"

Claudia's voice sounded different. "Starts at eight, so I'll send a car for you at seven-thirty if that's okay? It's at the Queen's Head pub. We'll all get cars back."

"I could get my own cab over."

"No, don't worry. Someone's passing your way, and it won't be a squad car to upset your nosey neighbours."

No use arguing with Claudia. She gave in graciously and ended the call. As Alesha would still be in school, she phoned her mum to confirm she was still free to babysit. Then she made an omelette before picking up Elizabeth from nursery.

TEN

ELIZABETH WAS IN bed by the time Alesha arrived to babysit at 7.15. Hannah had worked all day trying to make some order of what was in the third box. She had been carefully itemising everything and making different piles of things that were professional and those that related to Joan Ballantyne's private life. Sometimes the two overlapped. It was a mind-numbing task, trying to get things in date order so that she'd get an overview to work on.

She wondered if Leo had gone through any of this. Judging by his comment of wanting to get the funeral over and done with, she thought not. But why? Maybe he didn't trust himself to be objective. Plus, she supposed he was probably making the most of the time with his two little girls.

Thinking of them made her long for Elizabeth, so she finished up and went off to the nursery to collect her. She liked to vary her collection times so she could see what was going on when they weren't necessarily expecting her. She'd read somewhere that it was a good policy. It wasn't that she didn't trust the staff. She just wanted to be sure. Besides, it was always lovely to share some time together. It wouldn't take her long to get ready for the evening ahead and Elizabeth loved chatting and playing in her mummy's bedroom while she chose what to wear and got dressed.

"I'M NOT SURE what time I'll be back but I'll get a cab to take you home."

The girl laughed. "Don't worry. Dad will collect me. You know what he's like."

They shared a knowing smile. Sanjay Singh had become one of Hannah's champions and he loved the opportunity to say hello even if it was swiftly followed by a goodbye. After she'd returned from France, he, his wife and Alesha arrived with one of their very special home-cooked Indian meals for her. They didn't stay long, but it was obvious they wanted to make sure she was all right. "Think of me as an honorary uncle," Sanjay had said. "You must call us if you need anything."

Hannah felt she was the one being honoured.

The doorbell rang and Hannah checked the video camera. It took her a moment to recognise Sheridan James out of uniform. She looked stunning. Hannah felt drab in the black outfit she had chosen.

Alesha gave her a little push. "Off you go. You look great and we'll be fine."

Hannah smiled at her then went to open the door. Sheridan beamed at her. "Well you look so much better than the last time I saw you."

Hannah laughed. "That's not hard, seeing as I'd just been stabbed and…

Sheridan looked mortified. "I'm so sorry I didn't mean…

Hannah closed the door. "No I'm the one who should apologise. And thank you for being with me. So much of that day is a complete blur, but I do remember you holding my hand in the ambulance and your voice was so soothing and reassuring."

Sheridan had started the ignition. "Belt," she said sternly. "I need to get you to the party in one piece."

They both laughed and the tension passed, but Hannah's memories had dampened any enthusiasm she had for the party.

THE QUEEN'S HEAD pub was heaving when they arrived just before eight. Sheridan guided her to the bar where Claudia was ordering drinks. "White wine?"

Hannah nodded and was about to speak when a roar went up with banging on tables and clapping. Mike Benton, now DI Benton, had arrived. Hannah glanced at Claudia whose face looked a mixture of joy and then utter despair. Hannah knew how well they worked together and could understand Claudia's sense of loss.

Once Mike had a drink in his hand, someone blew a whistle and Claudia addressed the room. "I know Mike doesn't like long speeches so I'll be brief." A cheer went up. "Mike, I am going to miss your dogged determination to get to the bottom of a case. Your loyalty and willingness to go out on a limb. Your support and friendship. Your next team is so lucky to have you. And I for one am going to miss you dreadfully." She raised her glass and Hannah swallowed hard. She, too, had so much to thank Mike for, and then there was her chance as he stood before her.

"Hannah, I am so sorry I…"

"Mike, please don't apologise. You couldn't possibly have known and, I want to thank you for being a friend."

To save both embarrassing each other further they hugged awkwardly. Hannah thought she might cry, but was saved from any further conversation as Mike was whisked away by another colleague.

"Okay?" Claudia had come over with another drink. "I'm going to mingle a bit while I finish this, then I'm off. Don't want to cramp anyone's style. I'll give you a lift if you like." She moved away before Hannah, wondering why Claudia would be cramping anyone's style, could reply.

"Hello. Are you the journalist Mike keeps talking about? Hannah Weybridge?"

Hannah turned to the person who spoke. She was petite, pretty and wearing a stunning red dress which clung to her in all the right places. Her cheeks dimpled as she smiled.

"I am and don't tell me—you're Mike's wife!"

"That's right, Phoebe. I'm so pleased to see you're looking so well. Mike was gutted when—" she roared with laughter. "Sorry that really was a bad choice of phrase."

Hannah laughed. "You could say that, but it's much better than everyone pussy-footing around the injury. It's lovely to meet you Phoebe. A proud day for you."

"Yes I—"

Someone was calling for silence and Mike was hoisted up onto a table. He looked awkward but pleased. "I can't tell you how glad I am to be getting shot of you lot—" loud guffaws. "But there are three people here I'd like to say a special thank you to. Guv," He nodded at Claudia. "I would never have sat those exams if you hadn't prompted me. Thank you for your confidence in me and for not giving up on me when…" he paused, "when I wasn't functioning at my best. I have learned so much from you and hope I can be half as good at my job as you are." Claudia raised her glass to him.

Next to her Hannah could feel Phoebe tense. She looked as though she was willing herself to relax and smile.

"The second person is my beautiful and long-suffering wife."

A cheer went up in the room. "Without her… without her love and support, I might not have continued in the force. I'd probably have been kicked out. Phoebe you are the light of my life steering me onto safer shores."

The silence was sympathetic. "Which brings me to the third person. Hannah, when we first met I was going through a troubled time. And I wasn't exactly impressed by journalists."

Hannah wondered what the hell was coming next. The she felt a hand clutch hers and turned to see Phoebe smiling at her.

"Since then we have got to know each other better and—I think—we've become friends. Your investigations showed me another side to looking at things and I appreciate that as well as your bravery, determination and sheer bloody-mindedness." He paused. "So thank you Claudia, Phoebe and Hannah." He raised his glass. "And that's enough from me. There's a bar tab to drink dry!"

Hannah turned back to Phoebe, but she'd slipped away and she saw Mike put his arms around her shoulders and kiss her forehead. She felt a sharp stab of envy.

"Touching." Claudia was beside her. Hannah thought she was being sarcastic, then noticed her smile and what looked suspiciously like a tear forming in her eye. She finished her drink. "I'm leaving now. Can I give you a lift?" She correctly read Hannah's expression. "I have a driver waiting."

Without drawing any attention, they made their way through the throng and out of the pub. An unmarked car was waiting.

They both sat in the back seat and Hannah was going to be dropped off first. Neither spoke for a while; Hannah thought Claudia looked sad.

"Those events can get a bit rowdy and I'd only cramp their style."

"That's the second time you've said that. I'd have thought—" what she thought was lost when the driver swore loudly and applied the brakes so hard they screeched to a halt.

Outside Hannah's house there seemed to be some sort of scuffle. The driver who was in uniform, picked up his hat, got out of the car and walked slowly towards the two men involved, giving them time to acknowledge his presence.

"He's my best driver. Never gets stressed."

Hannah wondered about that as he'd just sworn. Then she realised Claudia was teasing her. "What have you got yourself into this time?"

"Would you believe a dead actress?"

Claudia didn't respond, but watched as the officer took down particulars and seemed to be admonishing the two men before they departed. "There's something I wanted to tell you but—" the officer was returning. "Now's not the time. When are you free for a chat and a takeaway, my treat?"

The officer opened the door for her. "Appears they were both waiting for your return and got into some sort of dispute over royalties, Ms Weybridge. They're both leaving now."

"Thank you."

"I got their cards as well, ma'am. For Ms Weybridge." He smiled. "Your editor might be able to report them to the PPC or something."

Hannah smiled her thanks and turned to Claudia. "Tomorrow? Eight suit you?" The other woman nodded and the car waited until she'd unlocked the door and gone inside.

"GOOD EVENING, HANNAH, I apologise for my intrusion into your home…" Sanjay Singh had stood up as Hannah entered the room.

Alesha was already standing, looking upset. "Hannah I'm so sorry. I called Dad when those men kept banging on the door and…"

"That's perfectly okay you did the right thing. I'm sorry you were exposed to this, Alesha. I'd been told the matter had been dealt with. Obviously not." Her furious expression made Mr Singh glad he was friend not foe.

Hannah reached into her handbag and pulled out an envelope she'd already prepared for her babysitter. She added another ten pounds. "For your inconvenience." She smiled. "I hope this won't put you off babysitting for me?"

"Oh no, as long as you don't mind if I phone my dad in emergencies?"

"Of course not. Although I hope there won't be any more. Thank you so much Sanjay. I'm sorry you were inconvenienced."

"Not at all, Hannah. Now come along Alesha. School tomorrow."

As they left, Hannah felt a sense of loneliness engulf her. Her scar itched. Always a bad sign. She locked up, drank some water and went upstairs. Looking in on her daughter always grounded her. Elizabeth murmured in her sleep and turned over.

Hannah went to the bathroom to shower off the smell of cigarette smoke from the pub. Not something she wanted to expose her daughter to. As the water flowed, her tears ran unchecked, unnoticed. She had to stop feeling sorry for herself like this.

TOM WAS WALKING towards her smiling. They met in a warm embrace but as they pulled apart it was Paul's face looking at her in concern. "Be careful…" She woke with a start, feeling bereft then she inhaled the smell of freesias. Her whole body relaxed as though wrapped in a shawl like a baby. Comforted, she drifted back to sleep.

ELEVEN

CLAUDIA ARRIVED A little after eight. "I called in at your favourite Indian and bring sustenance," she said, brandishing the take-away bags and producing a bottle of wine. She looked, as usual, immaculately groomed, but Hannah noticed there was something about her that was different—excited seemed too strong a word.

"You're a life saver. Just what I need after spending the day ploughing through Joan Ballantyne's paraphernalia."

"Oh?" Claudia's raised eyebrow said it all. They were in the kitchen. "Shall we eat in here?" She didn't wait for an answer, but started unpacking the tin-foil containers.

Hannah placed cutlery and glasses on the table and sat down opposite her guest. "Do you know anything about her death?"

"Her suicide? No only what I read in the papers. Why?"

"Just seemed strange, that's all. Ending your life on stage. Weird."

Claudia shrugged. "Maybe she was trying to make some sort of statement?"

"Perhaps."

They ate in silence for a few minutes.

"Supposing she was helped?"

Claudia paused in helping herself to some more chicken Jalfrezi. "What?" She sighed. "He's got to you hasn't he? The son?"

Hannah had the grace to blush.

"As I said, I read the papers…" Then she laughed. "You should see your face."

"Well he does have a point."

"And he's a rather attractive man. If you like that sort of thing."

Hannah contemplated Claudia's words. She had never spoken about partners. In fact, Hannah knew remarkably little about Claudia's personal life except that when they were training together at Hendon, Tom had got her out of a situation which could have ended her career before it had started. She had never shared the details.

"So what did you want to tell me?"

"Have you heard from Tom recently?"

Hannah had a feeling this wasn't what Claudia had been going to discuss with her. She hadn't heard from Tom and the longer the silence between them, the more she felt relieved. She had enjoyed their intimacy and there were times she thought it might lead to much more, but not now.

"No, I haven't. Have you?"

Claudia refilled their glasses. "Not directly." She sipped her wine. "Look, tell me to mind my own business, but I heard that he's been seeing someone in Australia and…"

It felt like the actual dagger that Peters had stabbed her with. The twist in her gut made her lean forward as she tried to compose herself. It was what she had sensed without knowing; what had haunted her dreams. She felt betrayed but not beaten. That he hadn't had the decency to tell her revealed his lack of commitment… alternatively maybe he thought he'd keep his options open, if and when he decided to return to the UK.

She reached for her drink and took a large gulp. "Thank you. Thank you for telling me."

"To be honest, I wasn't going to. I've known Tom a lot longer than you." She smiled to take away any unkindness in her words. "But I just thought…"

Claudia took another drink.

"Yes?"

"When I saw that photo of you and Leo Hawkins, it crossed my mind that you might be missing or ignoring opportunities for other relationships."

Hannah stared at her then laughed. "Are you trying to match-make, DI Turner?"

"No, I'm trying to be a friend."

"And you are. You're one of the few people I know who'll give up an evening to have a takeaway here…"

"That is no hardship believe me." That sounded heartfelt.

"Well, while we're on the subject, what about you? Any romantic interest?"

An infinitesimal pause. "Married to the job." There was a sad look in her eyes. "Anyway, going back to your question about Joan Ballantyne. There was nothing to suggest a suspicious death. Ms Ballantyne could have made that cocktail…"

"You checked it out?"

41

"I looked at the reports. I had an inkling you'd be asking me about her."

They contemplated each other for a moment then both laughed.

"Well, you seem to have my measure." Hannah topped up their glasses. "But could it have been? And the puff of smoke?"

Claudia finished the food on her plate. "As you have shown before, not all suicides have died by their own hand. What did Leo Hawkins have to say?"

"Off the record?" Claudia nodded. "He said, why would his mother fill her fridge with food and order a book if she intended to end her life?"

Claudia nodded. "A logical question, but suicides are rarely logical. Still, a strange place to end your life."

"Not really, if you think about it." Hannah was playing devil's advocate. "She spent most of her life either on stage or trying for another part to get her back there. Maybe it was payback time for those who had rejected her."

"Harsh. What was she like when you met her?"

Hannah paused considering. She had met her several times, always at her agent's office. It was as though she didn't want Hannah to see her personal space, which was odd since they were working on her biography. Caroline Maston Associates was situated in a Soho back street, above a Greek restaurant. The side door led into a well-lit hall, the walls of which were covered with pictures of their clients and a notice to the lift up to the suite of offices above. The reception area was overseen by an older woman who looked as though she might double as security. She appeared ferocious, but when she smiled—as she did when Hannah approached—her countenance changed to welcoming. Greta, as her desk nameplate indicated, led her into what might have been a small boardroom. Again the walls groaned under the weight of framed photographs. Caroline Maston, whom Hannah hadn't met before, stood up and held out her hand. She wore silk, fingerless gloves. Her clothes were immaculate and her demeanour haughty, as though Hannah were a mere minion who was imposing on her day in the ethereal world of show business.

"Delighted to meet you, Hannah. You come highly recommended."

Just then the door at the far end of the room opened and Joan Ballantyne, whom she recognised from her research, swept into the room. She brusquely shook Hannah's hand and dismissed her agent with a "Thank you, Caroline". Joan looked regal, but she had a sparkle that made Hannah think she was probably fun to be with in other circumstances. A soft grey dress flattered her figure; no rings adorned her fingers and her earrings were discreet, expensive-looking pearl studs to match her necklace.

Once they were alone, she unpacked a ream of type-written pages which had surprised Hannah as she'd assumed the actress would have dictated her thoughts. "I got my secretary to type my notes…" she must have interpreted Hannah's expression correctly and gave a girlish titter…" Well Lord Gyles got his secretary to do it for me. And it's all saved on floppy disks. Apparently you are far too important for such a mundane task." She'd stared at Hannah but not in an unfriendly way. "And, having read your exposés, I agree. Why on earth are you wasting your time with me, dear?"

Hannah came back to the present. "She was strange—patronising, and yet impressed by my journalism. She'd obviously done her homework on me. She said something quite odd about only really being alive when she was on stage."

"So why would you kill yourself where you feel most alive?"

"Exactly."

"And when's the funeral?"

"Tomorrow. Edith Holland's coming with me." Claudia looked at her quizzically. "The photographer. Lucy Peters' next-door neighbour."

"I know who she is. I'm surprised she's accompanying you."

"I got *The News* to use her as a freelance. She's good at fitting in and making herself almost invisible."

Claudia almost spat out her drink. "That's the last way I'd have described her."

Hannah gave her a withering look. "If it hadn't been for Edith's photos, I might never have got the lead on Edward Peters."

"Yes, you don't need to remind me." Claudia paused before asking, "You haven't seen Lucy?"

"No. Edith thinks she'd been spending more time at the Bull Ring, but as the weather cools, she'll probably make her way back to the flat."

They had finished their meal and Claudia glanced at her watch. "Better book a cab. Early start tomorrow."

RINSING THE PLATES before putting them in the dishwasher, Hannah went over her conversation with Claudia. It must have taken a lot for her to tell Hannah about Tom, considering how close they were, or had been. Of course, it could be just rumour, but Hannah didn't think so. Claudia was far too astute to report gossip. Maybe Tom had had someone when he was working in New York as well. A woman in every port? It made her feel sick that she'd allowed herself to be deceived, but her rational side defended him. She had more or less refused to see him after the Peters debacle. He had not been straight with her. Maybe his job meant he never would be. That was not the sort of relationship she wanted. If she wanted a relationship at all. She had Elizabeth. Paul hadn't been honest with her, either. Maybe it was the nature of the beast. She hoped not. She giggled at the thought of Claudia pairing her with Leo Hawkins. Although he had been married with two children, she was almost convinced he was gay. She'd known Joe for long enough to know the signs. She drank a glass of water and peered out into the darkened garden, just glimpsing a large fox walking along the wall. As though sensing her interest, the fox paused and seemed to look directly at her. An acknowledgment. Somehow that was reassuring; the fox patrolling her garden, keeping guard. A fanciful idea. She went upstairs with a smile on her face.

TWELVE

IF THERE WAS one thing Hannah would rather she had not got used to, it was attending funerals. In such a short time she had been to Caroline's, Liz's, Father Patrick's memorial, Lucy's brother's and now Joan Ballantyne's. This was much more on a par with Liz's, and Hannah, after their conversation when she visited them, wasn't surprised to see Celia Rayman and Mary there, although they were way in front of her in the line.

It was a ticketed affair and there was a queue into St Paul's in Covent Garden, known affectionately as the Actors' Church. The paved area before the entrance and garden beds all looked amazing in the autumnal sunshine. Dressed for the occasion. Eventually, she and Edith moved up the line to the doors to have their invitations scrutinised by the security people Leo Hawkins had seen fit to employ. Hannah wondered if it was really necessary and also noticed there were mounted police in attendance on Bedford Street. Perhaps they were there for crowd control—there was an amazingly large number of people crowding at the railings in front of the churchyard. Joan's fans? Or perhaps people who loved to celebrity spot? Edith slipped her arm through Hannah's and gave it a reassuring squeeze. She was totally unfazed by the gathering, and fitted in perfectly with her flamboyant style and purple hair, as guests had been requested to wear their favourite colours.

Set back from the curated line of guests was a bank of photographers. Hannah knew there'd be one from *The News* and all the major UK and foreign news outlets.

Edith had surveyed them, her expression giving nothing away. "Motley crew, aren't they?"

Hannah didn't look. She had no wish to draw attention to herself. She concentrated on the mourners. She recognised so many famous faces, but not others who looked important: the moneymen, directors and producers. Many looked genuinely sad. She wondered how many were asking themselves if they could have done something more, been there for Joan to prevent her death. And another niggle edged its way into her thoughts. If she hadn't taken her own life, was Joan's killer here? And if so, how would she ever be able to expose him or her?

INSIDE THE CHURCH the atmosphere was almost festive. There was a sense of people checking who else was there. See and be seen was the order of the day. Some were waving and blowing kisses across the pews. The music was from *The Boy Friend*, a musical Joan had starred in many years ago. Leo had wanted the service to be as upbeat as possible, to be a celebration of his mother's life and achievements. Many in the pews hummed along to the tunes.

The music changed as the organist played the opening chords from Elgar's *Lux Aeterna* and everyone stood as the choir's voices rang out with a sense of gravitas. Then the priest's deep, solemn voice intoned the opening words of the service: "'I am the resurrection and the life,' saith the Lord; 'he that believeth in me, though he were dead, yet shall he live; and whosoever liveth and believeth in me shall never die,'" as he led the cortege to the front of the church. Leo held hands with both his daughters. The two little girls looked awestruck by the architecture of the church.

Hannah wondered if Joan had believed in God. Her generation was more likely to. What about her son? It was convenient at the end of a life to cling on to the thought that this was not the end. The best was yet to come. She was only half listening to the priest as she tuned into whispered comments she overheard. Surreptitiously, she made notes in the order of service when several of Joan's oldest friends reflected on her life. Then Leo stood and the raw grief he expressed stunned the congregation into silence and then, like a practiced raconteur, he brought the house down as he told a wonderful, funny story about his mother.

From behind her Hannah heard someone say, sotto voce, "Crocodile tears if you ask me."

"Shush."

"Well, I mean how many times did he visit her, I wonder?"

The reply was lost as the organist played the opening chords of Fauré's *Pie Jesu* and everyone stood as the coffin was taken out. As the congregation turned to the rear, Hannah caught sight of the person who had spoken and took a couple of photos with her concealed camera. These were for her reference only.

LEO HAWKINS AND the family, including Joan's younger sister, Eileen, and her husband, Leo's ex-wife and two daughters, left with the coffin and there was much milling around in the garden in front of the church. A fleet of black cabs had been hired to take the invited guests to the wake at The Old Vic in Waterloo. Hannah and Edith contrived to be near the front of the queue so they would be in the advance party. It would give them time to position themselves and watch the other guests and mourners as they arrived. Edith took out the badge Leo had had made for her which told everyone she was the Official Photographer. Hannah wondered why he had done this. It seemed unnecessary. She had noticed how many guests had been posing for the press corps. Second nature, she assumed, for people who spent their lives in front of cameras or on stage. Then she watched in astonishment as an elderly actor who she couldn't put a name to clutched his chest and looked as though he was going to pass out. Two people were instantly either side of him, supporting him. The cameras clicked in a noisy battery and quite a few people looked furious that they had been upstaged.

"Five to a cab, please."

Hannah and Edith were pushed forward into the taxi and found themselves on the fold down seats in front of two women and a man who looked disgruntled more than sad. "Did you see that primped up pansy and his dying swan act?"

"Shush Gavin. Don't get yourself in a state. It's not good for you."

"Nor is he, the…

"Oh for goodness sake can't you leave off the carping and show some respect?" The third passenger who just spoke was someone Hannah had no difficulty in recognising.

"Hello Caroline. How are you coping? Must be a nightmare for you."

Caroline Maston, Joan Ballantyne's agent, glared at her before addressing her fellow mourners. "This is Hannah Weybridge, a journalist—" she emphasised the word as though issuing a warning about something unsavoury. "And, until recently, collaborating with Joan on her autobiography."

There was an awkward pause. As though someone should say something but could think of nothing. Hannah pondered the "until recently".

"And I'm Edith Holland. Leo asked me to take photographs at the wake."

"How distasteful." Caroline looked down her nose at Edith. "And you'll be selling them afterwards I suppose. How tacky."

They were crossing Waterloo Bridge. Hannah saw that Edith's attention was focused on Caroline's hands. She was wearing fingerless, black silk gloves and her nails—talons, thought Hannah—were blood red, matching her scarf. Now that she thought about it, on every occasion Hannah had seen her, Caroline always wore fingerless gloves. She wondered if she had a disfigurement.

"No more tacky than you going through all her film credits and trying to get a retrospective on TV before she was hardly cold," said the man. "I'm Gavin Young by the way, and this is my wife Gwen."

Hannah thought she ought to know the name but nothing sprang to mind. Certainly he wasn't someone Joan had talked about. She was saved from making a comment by Caroline's sharp, "Well, here we are."

The taxi driver got out and opened the door. Obviously Edith and Hannah had to get out first and that seemed to annoy the agent as well. Perhaps she had been planning on a grand entrance at the theatre. A group of fans and photographers had gathered, held back by some temporary railings and a few security men.

Caroline adjusted her emerald green cape and entered the theatre with a flourish, but Gavin Young, arm-in-arm with his wife, paused to sign a few autographs. Hannah noticed how he spoke quietly and kindly to each person and then she remembered who he was. He played the local GP in *Chicory Road* and he had adopted that persona for the well-wishers. Never off duty, Hannah thought, and wondered why Caroline had been so put out at seeing her or sharing a taxi with her. Agents weren't supposed to steal the limelight, but Joan's death must have had peculiar repercussions on her life.

MANY PEOPLE HAD been surprised that the wake would be held in the very theatre where Joan Ballantyne had died, but in fact the Lilian Baylis Bar was perfect. Champagne and canapés made the round of guests. Hannah was amused to see how little some ate, watching their figures presumably, and how much was consumed by others, whose bodies told their own story.

Edith had deserted her as she made her way through the ever-increasing throng to take her photos. She had a small Dictaphone with her as she asked people for their names. Some, Hannah learned later, had also given their contact details for copies of prints.

"Thank you for being here, Hannah." She was startled by Leo Hawkins, who had arrived without ceremony. "I have to talk to people, but I'd like you to join me so I can introduce you as my mother's biographer. That might get them to open up to you."

He must have noticed Hannah's startled expression. "It's okay. I cleared this with Lord Gyles. We agreed that letting people know there would be an officially sanctioned biography would probably put off a lot of others and we have lawyers ready to fire off warning letters to anyone thinking of breaching copyright and embargoes."

His smile was weary and, for a moment, his expression was utterly bleak. This quickly transformed when he was slapped on the back by a tall, lean, grey-haired man. "Perfect eulogy, Leo. You did your mother proud. So sad she couldn't confide in any of us how she was feeling…"

Hannah recognised Sir David Powys, renowned actor and writer who sat on various public committees, as well as directing *Lady Heston Regrets*. Leo looked as though he was going to disagree, and then thought the better of it. He smiled. "May I introduce you to Hannah Weybridge, my mother's official biographer? Excuse me." Hannah was startled that he had just left her there.

Sir David's smile curdled. "A new departure for you, is it not, Ms Weybridge?"

"I'm sorry?" Hannah's antennae were on full alert.

"Writing biographies." He paused as though to allow for his words to take effect. "After your investigative journalism for *The News*, I mean. I trust you have fully recuperated?"

The extent of Hannah's injuries sustained during the apprehension of Edward Peters had never been made public. She wondered how much he knew and how. She had already taken a photo of him from her lapel camera.

"I'm very well, thank you." She sipped her drink. "Were you close to Joan? It must have been a shock—the way she died."

"Yes." He stared at someone or something behind her. Just for a moment his face reflected what she thought was true sadness, soon replaced by a shuttered expression, which brooked no breach. "But nothing to excite your spurious interest."

"Darling David, how naughty of you to monopolise Ms Weybridge—I need her to meet someone." Sir David inclined his head and Hannah felt herself propelled across the rapidly filling room. "Such a bore," said the blonde-haired woman in her mid-sixties, wearing scarlet lipstick, a mass of eye make-up and sporting an outfit that shrieked haute couture and fit her like a glove. Actress Diana Stowbridge needed no introduction. She guided Hannah to a table with two seats miraculously unoccupied, and nodded to a waiter. Fresh glasses of champagne arrived along with a plate of canapés.

As they sat, she clasped Hannah's hand. "I was one of Joan's closest friends and I don't believe for one moment that she killed herself, no matter what the police or anyone else say. I didn't want to say anything to Leo—he's heartbroken you know—but I'm determined to get to the bottom of this, and I know you can help me."

Hannah sipped her champagne. "How do you know that, Miss Stowbridge?"

"Diana, please. Because I am also a friend of Lady Celia Rayman."

Hannah smiled. "Don't tell me, you went to drama school together?" Hannah had looked around but Celia and Mary had not joined the party here.

The actress gave her an arch look. "We did as a matter of fact. Now, here's my card and I'd be most grateful if you'd phone me to arrange a time to meet up…"

"Di-ana, darling. What are you doing tucked away in this corner?"

Hannah's whole body tensed. She recognised the voice and the echo of a threat but couldn't place it.

"Jim, sweetheart this is Hannah. We have a friend in common. Hannah it was lovely meeting you." And with that she clutched Jim's arm and allowed herself to be led away. Hannah was grateful for the reprieve. Then Jim turned back towards her.

"Maybe we have a friend in common too?"

Her smile froze. She knew without a doubt this was the person who'd left a message on her answerphone about Joan's obituary.

Instinctively she would not trust someone who didn't leave his name. Seeing him in person did nothing to dispel the idea.

Hannah felt exhausted. Being in a crowd of unfamiliar people—or even familiar people—sent ripples of remembered fear throughout her body. She deliberately slowed her breathing and thought of her daughter whose image always relaxed her. There really was no point in her being at the funeral. There were so many people that she would never be able to distinguish who was in the cast and crew of Joan Ballantyne's last play and who were friends from a lifetime in the theatre. She recognised some and hadn't a clue about others.

She managed to talk to Coral Moore and Roger Priest, though neither could cast any light on what had happened. Hannah thought there was something about Roger. He was clearly agitated and she wondered if he took drugs.

"Joan's death must have been such a shock for you." She'd hoped her voice sounded sympathetic, but his reply was terse.

"Of course it was. What a bloody stupid question." He walked away, pulling Coral in his wake.

"Do sit down, you look as though you're about to collapse."

Hannah turned to see Edith beside her. "I think we could go soon. I've got masses of photos and some tasty titbits of gossip." She grinned. "Best day's work I've had for ages."

"Well, I'm glad you're been successful. I feel a total fraud being here."

Edith gave her a look she couldn't fathom. "I need to get to my studio to develop these films and match up the notes. Where would you like to meet up tomorrow to go through them?"

"Why don't you both join me at my mother's apartment tomorrow afternoon, if that's not too soon for you, Edith?" It was Leo Hawkins' voice. "It might be interesting for you to have a wander around the place, Hannah. And with a bit of luck, it will be the last place anyone will think of staking out."

"Okay." Hannah had never seen Edith so compliant.

Leo gave her the address. "See you there. Two o'clock?" As she left, Hannah saw her pause to talk to various people. She'd been right to invite Edith. She fitted in superbly. A chameleon.

"Now let me get you a taxi."

"No, I don't need to draw any more attention to myself. I'll see you tomorrow." She shook Leo's hand and made her way through the thinning throng. Just as she reached the door, she heard her name. Or rather she heard someone talking about her. "... she's that journalist whose investigations have upset a lot of people in high places."

"Surely that's a good thing, isn't it? Exposing ..."

"Don't be so naïve. The real people involved never get exposed. There's always someone there to cover for them. I even heard that..."

Hannah heard no more as they had moved away from earshot. She felt alone and out of sorts and left the theatre with a sense of foreboding although she couldn't think why.

As she got into the cab, she stared across at Drayton House where Lucy lived—or perhaps not, if Edith was right. She knew she'd have to meet with her at some point, but not yet. Certainly not today, when she felt so raw...

The driver was one of those who loved to chat. "At Joan Ballantyne's funeral were you?" He looked at her in the rearview mirror as she nodded. "Should I recognise you? Been in anything big lately?"

Hannah laughed. "Not at all. I'm not an actress." He looked crestfallen. "Just a friend of the family."

He nodded. "'Spect there were loads of big names there, though?"

"Yes there were." Give him a crumb, Hannah thought, aware that she was a disappointment. "I chatted to Diana Stowbridge."

"Now there's a lady. Good actress too. Loved her in..."

Hannah tuned out, but he didn't seem to notice as he commented on some of Diana Stowbridge's greatest roles. Surreptitiously she checked her phone. There were no messages. She realised the driver had stopped talking and was looking at her expectantly. She was home. She paid and tipped him well. "Need a receipt?"

"Yes please." She smiled her thanks and watched him drive off. Her street was mercifully quiet. She'd check her emails and then collect Elizabeth from nursery.

There was only one email. From Rory. "Hope the funeral wasn't too much of an ordeal. Our outside photographer caught Tom Diamond in full OTT mode..." So that's who he was. He would probably be on all the front pages tomorrow much to the chagrin of a host of other actors.

THIRTEEN

HANNAH HAD BEEN intrigued when Edith had phoned the next morning to suggest they meet at her studio before seeing Leo Hawkins at his mother's home. She was happy to oblige. The studio was under the arches by Waterloo Station. Hannah had never been there before and was curious. The walls in Edith's flat were covered with her artwork, which Hannah found too bright and colourful for her taste, but she had reason to be grateful for her photography— both professionally and personally. Edith had a knack of capturing scenes and people without them being aware. Photos of the then unknown killer Edward Peters, who had been following Harry Peters, had been crucial in finally uncovering his crimes.

Edith welcomed her in with a broad smile. "Coffee?"

Hannah nodded, looking around her with interest. The 'studio' was, in fact, several rooms. Where she worked on her art was behind another door that Edith didn't open. There was also a dark room and the area they were in, which was a workroom plus somewhere to take photos if necessary. In contrast to where Edith lived, this room was monochrome. They sat at a table and Edith brought out a folder of photographs.

"I sent the contact sheets and some prints to *The News* this morning. These photos—" she fanned them out, "are, I think, of particular interest to you."

Hannah sat forward and scrutinised them surprised to see that she appeared in several. One was of her, Diana Stowbridge and Jim whose surname she hadn't discovered.

Edith pointed a finger at him. "James Fentonbury. Kept track of you the whole time."

"Really?" Hannah was stunned. Then remembered he was probably the mystery caller who had left a message of her answerphone.

Edith showed her a few more prints. He was never more than a few people away from her and he had obviously kept her in his sights.

"How strange."

Edith gave her an odd look, but kept whatever thoughts she had on the subject to herself. "I've made you up a full set of prints here. Clipped to them are their contact details and any snippets of conversation we had. Thought it might help."

"Help? You're a star, Edith. This is brilliant. Thank you." Hannah was itching to open the file and read Edith's comments, but knew they didn't have the time. Edith picked up another envelope; her camera bag was by the door ready.

"Shall we go?"

THEY TOOK A taxi to Clifton House. It was an imposing Georgian building, which had been converted into large apartments. A concierge greeted them in the marble tiled foyer. He consulted a diary he had on his desk.

"Miss Edith Holland and Miss Hannah Weybridge?" They nodded. "Please sign the visitors' book." Hannah wondered if that was absolutely necessary. She took her time signing, so she could use her hidden camera to photograph the names on the page above Edith's signature. "Mr Hawkins is waiting for you in Miss Ballantyne's apartment. Please take the lift to the first floor." As the women did as they were bid, they heard the concierge ring Leo to tell him that his guests were on their way.

Hannah had wondered why they hadn't been given an apartment number but before she could ponder more, the lift came to a halt and opened directly on to a vestibule, which was obviously part of Joan Ballantyne's residence. A door opened and Leo stood before them. He looked harassed.

"Is this a bad time, Leo? We could come back."

Edith glared at her. No they couldn't.

"No. No. Come through." He stepped aside for them to enter a spacious, beautifully furnished drawing room. Heavy red velvet drapes adorned huge, floor-to-ceiling windows, which looked out onto what must be a shared garden. The room was full of light and, Hannah felt, happiness. However, from Leo's demeanour, it was evident that something was wrong.

"I'm sorry Hannah, Edith. Please sit down. He motioned to the chairs placed round a table. "I got here just a short while ago and it seems as though someone else has been in the apartment."

"Is anything missing that you are aware of?" Hannah's stomach tightened. She experienced an undercurrent of fear. Her scar itched.

Leo ran his hands through his hair and Hannah noticed the grey strands. "I don't know. There's just a sense of... I don't know, a disturbance. Sounds daft, I know."

Edith's was the voice of cool reason. "Why don't we walk around the apartment, and I'll take photographs of any areas where you think something seems different. It might help you remember."

He looked relieved at having something constructive to do. "Thank you."

"Have you asked the concierge if anyone else has been here?" Hannah asked. "Or perhaps he has been into the apartment?"

"No, he hasn't, and he says no one else has. But come over here."

They followed him to some French windows, which led onto a balcony. The area was huge. Lots of well-tended pot plants, a bistro-type table and chairs and, at the far end, a gate to a spiral staircase leading to the garden.

"When I came in, I heard a noise. The French windows hadn't been shut properly. My mother always locked them."

"You were here the other day packing up papers to be delivered to me. Did you open the window then?"

"No, but I did check all the doors and windows were locked when I left."

Edith had been snapping away with her camera. She said little, but Hannah sensed she was observing everything closely and making mental notes.

"Shall we take a walk around the apartment now?" Her suggestion was met with a nod and Hannah was aware how carefully he locked the doors once they were back inside.

The apartment was huge, but it was obvious that, at least of late, only a few rooms had been in use. Edith took her photographs and Hannah took a few of her own with her concealed camera. She also made some notes on a pad as they went around. All of the rooms led off a wide, central hallway. It was akin to being in a picture gallery with all the framed photos and artwork from theatre posters and programmes. A fascinating pictorial life story. Joan Ballantyne's personal hall of fame.

"Is this how your mother left her bedroom?" Hannah was shocked. It threw a completely different light on the actress beloved of so many. The king size bed was unmade, a silk wrap had been thrown to the floor, an empty coffee cup was on the bedside table along with bottles of pills, sundry pieces of jewellery, a photograph of her with one of the Knights, used tissues… Her dressing table was strewn with makeup containers, cotton wool, a hairbrush that looked as though it hadn't been cleaned for an age, more pieces of jewellery, a notebook and pen.

Hannah picked up the pen and used it to flip open the notebook. Some pages had been torn out, but Hannah recognised several names and key words on other pages. "May I take this with me?"

Leo barely glanced at what she was referring to. "Of course." His attention was focused across the room on a pile of clothes presumably worn the day before she died. Hannah had no idea what he was thinking but his thoughts must have been painful from his expression as he stood at the door. "I couldn't face coming in here. She has—had—a woman who comes in three times a week and clears up after her. I'm afraid my mother thought she was above such things."

"Do you have contact details for her?"

"Yes I can email them to you."

"Had she been working for your mother for long?"

Leo shrugged. "I have no idea."

In the silence that ensued the lens shutter on Edith's camera sounded loudly intrusive. Her face was unreadable. Leo looked embarrassed.

"I suppose it would be difficult to tell if anything had been moved or taken from this room?" Hannah's question seemed insensitive even to her own ears.

Leo was silent for a moment. "The photograph." The word came out on a sigh.

Edith and Hannah stared at him, as he had turned seriously pale. "Someone has inverted the photograph of me. Look." He pointed to the other bedside table, which was less cluttered. A silver frame took pride of place, but the photograph of a young boy in school uniform had been taken out and turned upside down. Edith moved closer to take another photograph.

Hannah took out a handkerchief and gingerly picked up the frame. "Do you have a clean bag?"

Without a word, Leo left the room and returned moments later with a freezer bag. "Will this do?"

"Perfect." Hannah placed the frame in the bag and put it into her briefcase. "Anything else you can see wrong with this room?"

"No. I don't know. It's not somewhere I've been to recently." He looked defeated. "If my mother had decided to kill herself, she definitely wouldn't have left her room like this." He seemed to have forgotten Edith's presence. "She would be furious that anyone would see this less than perfect side to her life."

Hannah tended to agree. Not many women would literally air their dirty linen in public. Especially not a woman as vain as Hannah had considered Joan Ballantyne to be. "Shall we go through to the bathroom?"

Edith preceded them into the en suite, which was the size of Elizabeth's bedroom, and took photos. Towels on the floor, a smear of toothpaste on the hand basin, hair clogging the plughole in the shower. Not the state of a room to be inspected after you'd died. It really didn't add up. Alternatively, if she *had* decided to end her life, maybe she cared nothing about the chaos she'd be leaving behind her?

Leo had come back to the present. "Let me show you the kitchen."

As Hannah walked back through the bedroom, a shaft of sunlight caught something on the floor. She bent down, photographed it then used a pen to pick up the gold chain. A heavy locket hung open and empty. No photograph in either side. But there obviously had been once, as Hannah caught sight of a tiny piece of photographic paper caught within the frame.

"Leo?" He paused in the doorway. "Do you know whose photos your mother kept in her locket?"

He looked about to cry. "God I haven't seen that for years. There was a photo of me and I think the other side held one of my father."

They walked down the hall and into a room at the end, which was a bright, modern kitchen that looked as though it was rarely used. Leo opened a drawer and passed her another freezer bag without having to be asked. Hannah placed the locket inside. Everything was clean and tidy. Only a used coffee cup in the sink to break the spell. Leo opened the fridge.

"You see. Full of food."

Edith took photos of packages of food rapidly reaching their use by date. It hadn't seemed to occur to him that the food would be going off and should be thrown away. "And the freezer… and cupboards."

Hannah was thoughtful. "It was a matinée on the day your mother died, Leo. Would she have had breakfast or lunch here before she left?" Hannah was remembering the coffee cup in Joan's bedroom.

He shrugged. "In my memory she only ever had coffee for breakfast. She wouldn't have eaten much before a performance, so maybe she had something light in her dressing room at the theatre."

Edith had finished taking shots. Hannah took out another handkerchief. "Do you have another of those freezer bags?" Leo looked at her questioningly. "If your mother had already had her coffee, this may have been used by the person who came here."

THREE OTHER ROOMS seemed untouched. Dust sheets over furniture, curtains half-drawn. The still air of the unused. There was a forlornness about them.

"The only other room is my mother's study. I went in there to collect her files and memorabilia for you Hannah. Would you like to see the room?"

"Yes please." Hannah had almost forgotten Edith was there. She smiled at her. She knew how she loved to create a photographic world to tell a story. This would be the last piece of the jigsaw.

"Shit." Leo had opened the door and stepped back. Someone had made short work of any order that the room may have had. Drawers were open, files thrown to the floor; a paperweight had been hurled across the room. For a moment Hannah stood there absorbing the frenzied chaos. She could feel the anger, resentment and disappointment the room had been testament to. No one said a word. Edith's camera shutter was the only sound.

"Leo I think you ought to call the police."

They all stepped out of the study. Leo shut the door and they walked back into the drawing room. He made the call.

"Would you mind if I didn't wait with you?" Edith looked torn between leaving and staying. "I'd like to get back to process these prints and I have another client this afternoon."

Leo smiled. The first time since they had arrived. "Of course not and thank you so much for your time and the photos from the funeral. I'll look at them later." He saw her to the lift and then returned to where Hannah was standing admiring a portrait of his mother. "That was done by Thomas Fielding. I think he was more than a little in love with her."

"It shows." Hannah suspected it was a mutual feeling. Joan Ballantyne's expression was soft, inviting, sensual. She must have been in her forties when it was painted. It occurred to her that maybe her expression wasn't for the painter but for someone else who had been in the room.

"Would you like some coffee?" Hannah nodded and they moved back into the kitchen.

"Shall we sort this fridge out?" Hannah suggested as Leo filled the kettle.

"Good idea." He opened a draw and produced a black sack, which they proceeded to fill with the contents of the fridge. "That's odd."

"What is?"

"These prawns. My mother hated them so why would she buy them?"

"Maybe she was having someone to supper."

"Perhaps." Leo didn't look convinced.

The internal phone rang which Leo answered. "Thank you. Please send them up. Excuse me. The police have arrived."

FOURTEEN

AN HOUR LATER, Hannah had given her statement and handed over the cup and the photo-frame in their freezer bags. The male officer had given her a strange look, but the woman with him smiled at her. Hannah had the feeling she knew who she was. When they saw the state of the study, one of them radioed their station and asked for a scene of crimes officer. Hannah had her prints taken "for elimination purposes" even though she assured them she was on their database.

"I need to call the office," she told Leo. She was about to accept the offer to use his mother's phone when she remembered how it had been drilled into her to call on her "safe" line at all times. She smiled and walked away to the French windows.

Her call went straight through to the editor. "There's been a development. Someone has been into Joan Ballantyne's study and ransacked it. Do you think all the documents will be safe at my house?"

Georgina was quiet for a moment. "I'll get back to you Hannah. Where are you now?"

"I'm at Joan's apartment with her son. Edith has not long left."

"Right stay there until you hear from me." With that she hung up.

Hannah joined the others, who were talking about security. There was a buzz from the lift and one of the police officers went out to open the door.

A man walked into the room. Hannah stared at him. He nodded at her then introduced himself to Leo. "DI Benton, Mr Hawkins. I've spoken to the concierge and it seems your mother had had no visitors for a week or so apart from her cleaner. So we must assume whoever entered the apartment did so via the steps from the garden." He walked over to the French windows and inspected the lock. "Simple enough to open this." He smiled at Hannah. "Need to get your security people in, Hannah."

Leo and the two officers looked at her curiously, but she was saved from responding by the ringing of her phone and moved away to answer it. Georgina sounded unusually flustered.

"Hi Hannah—I've had a chat with Lord Giles and our lawyer, and they both think the documents should be fine at your home, given your security arrangements. However, as a precaution we're going to send Securicor to your home to collect the boxes. Just put anything in them. We'll make quite a performance of collecting them, just in case anyone is watching your home. My driver is already on his way to collect you and will take you home. He'll supervise the collection. You can trust him. I'll speak to you again tomorrow." She hung up.

Hannah went over to the others just as the internal phone rang. Leo answered it. "A car has arrived for you Hannah." He smiled and kissed her cheek. "I'll call you."

"You know where to find me, Inspector." She smiled at the DI.

Benton returned her smile. "I do indeed."

Leo escorted her to the lift and within a few minutes she was ensconced in the editor's car. Her driver maintained a silence, for which she was grateful.

He accompanied her into the house and helped her pack magazines and old newspapers into the boxes she'd kept ready to return Joan Ballantyne's things.

When the driver from Securicor arrived he handed the boxes to him. He'd hardly said a word the whole time they were together. Hannah didn't know whether to feel relieved or intimidated by his silence.

As he left, a smile lit up his face. "Don't let the bastards get you down, Hannah. If they're trying to scare you, it means they have something to hide." And with that he left the house and drove away.

AFTER COLLECTING ELIZABETH from nursery, Hannah spent some time playing with her in the bath and reading stories. She missed having Janet in the house. Another adult to rely on. Elizabeth was tired and cranky. In the end, she fell asleep in her mother's arms, her cheeks flushed. Hannah hoped she wasn't sickening for something. Attending a nursery meant she was exposed to a larger variety of germs. But she loved playing with the other children there, and Hannah had met and liked some of the parents.

In fact Elizabeth had been invited to a birthday party on Saturday and Hannah was looking forward to it, in spite of feeling apprehensive. Then there was lunch with Celia and Mary. Her social life was looking up. Gently she placed Elizabeth in her cot and crept out of the room.

GLASS OF WINE in hand, she took the file Edith had given her into the dining room. She placed the groups of photos in the order Edith had suggested. Each one had a note indicating who was in the shots and some had cryptic comments attached to them, which Hannah only glanced at, hoping to catch the bigger picture.

Actors, it seemed, took funerals seriously. Especially when it was for one of the "grand dames" of the theatre. Edith had added times to the photos as well. In those at the beginning, marking the arrivals from St Paul's, faces looked genuinely saddened. Some looked grief-stricken. Others perplexed. There was one of herself looking tired and lost. As time progressed people looked more animated. Sharing good memories, she hoped. It took on the air of a first night party as the champagne flowed.

Hannah went up to her study to fetch her magnifying glass. Coming back down the stairs, she thought she saw a shadow at the door. She went into the sitting room where she'd left the portable viewing screen. No one showed. Then she noticed an envelope had been pushed through the letterbox.

For a moment, she just stood there staring at its whiteness. Her name had been written in capitals along with "By Hand". Hannah picked it up and walked into the dining room. The envelope was postcard size and felt flimsy. She opened it and took out a single sheet of paper.

"Dear Hannah. You don't know me but I live next-door but one to you. In the last day or so, I've noticed that someone in the house opposite, number 5, has been taking photographs from the upstairs window. Whoever it is seems to be focusing on your house. I just thought you might like to know.

Best wishes, Hazel Smith." Hazel had also added her telephone number.

Hannah could feel the anxiety building up in her body and settling like lead. Her vulnerability was only too obvious. Maybe she should think about moving house. The very thought of packing up, finding somewhere to live and all that that entailed horrified her. Her security was tight. She knew that. But nowhere was completely impenetrable if someone was really determined.

In the dining room she took a gulp of her wine and tried to concentrate on the photos. Edith had done a brilliant job, not only of identifying everyone, but she'd also highlighted the cast and crew of Joan Ballantyne's last appearance. And there were telephone numbers.

Hannah made a list of those and the order in which she would contact them on Monday. She felt rather a fraud as Edith had done so much of the research. She looked again at the photos of James Fentonbury—Jim as Diana Stowbridge had introduced him. Wherever he was, Edith was right, he was certainly watching her. She'd had an instinctive aversion to him, convinced that he'd left the unpleasant message on her answerphone. Then, as she was examining the photos, she caught one expression, which brought her up short. He was definitely looking at her as she could see herself in the photo, talking to Leo. His expression was... concerned. He looked as though he wanted to protect her. From what? Leo? Hannah brushed away the fanciful thoughts and looked at the photos Edith had grouped together as cast and crew.

The play, *Lady Heston Regrets*, had only six characters—so five at the wake, plus the two understudies. Three women and four men. Edith had attached their names and the parts they played, along with a few comments. Coral Moore and Roger Priest she knew were on stage for the discovery. That left Adrian Brown, Mark Webster and Gwen Owens. She studied the photos they appeared in. No clues there.

The backstage crew was more numerous: all of them looked... haunted was the word she would have chosen. But that was fanciful too. Sad. They were sad and after all it was a sad occasion. Hannah flipped through ASM, make-up and wigs, lighting, sound, props... The director.

An image hit her so hard she couldn't breathe. Why hadn't she seen him there? And why hadn't he seen her? Or if he had seen her, why had he avoided her? What the hell was Sam Smith doing working in a theatre? Surely there was no call for a lost property clerk at The Old Vic?

Nothing made sense. Or at least no sense she could fathom. And the note from her neighbour had unsettled her more than she'd like to admit.

When she went upstairs to bed, she didn't turn on the light but edged around the room to the window and stared out. Lights were on in Leah's house. Closed curtains in the windows of number seven. But she could just make out a small glimmer in the window of number five. Was someone watching her right now? And if so what on earth was he after?

FIFTEEN

EARLY THE NEXT morning, she rang Mike Benton. He wasn't available—it was a Saturday—so she left a message. She then rang *The News* but Georgina wasn't there. Rory was.

"How easy would it be to find out if someone was in a stakeout opposite my home and taking photos of me or what's going on at my house?" She asked without preamble.

"Leave it with me." He didn't ask anything or offer any reassurances, Hannah noticed, but she felt better having passed the baton. She could rely on Rory. He had never let her down.

Hannah realised how restricted her social life had become when a children's party was a special occasion. Elizabeth attending the nursery in the next road meant they were meeting more local families. She wondered what the etiquette was. She had a present for Harry—the birthday boy. It was a game she'd chosen for its lack of stereotyping, called Tummy Ache. It required little skill but was, she hoped, fun to play. Should Elizabeth wear a party frock? Should she? Did she need to dress to impress?

She knew so few people in the area that she hadn't a clue about children's parties. In desperation she'd rung Linda, whom she hadn't seen since the autumn term had begun.

"Oh, just wear something you're comfortable in and which you don't mind having children spill stuff on." She laughed. "It's no big deal, you know."

"It is for me." They chatted for a while before Linda rang off with a "Remember to relax and enjoy yourself." And with that Hannah had to be satisfied.

At least the home of the birthday boy was only a few streets away. Elizabeth seemed subdued in the buggy but when they arrived, she screeched: "Harry" and gave him a big hug. They did a little jig of joy and he took her hand as they both went into the sitting room.

The house was similar to Hannah's—a Victorian terrace. The place had a comfortable, lived-in feel about it and Fran, whom she'd met several times at the nursery, gave her a welcome hug. "I'm so glad you could make it. Harry is beyond himself with excitement and hasn't stopped asking when Elizabeth would be here."

Hannah smiled. "They do look very happy to see each other."

There were, it transpired, seven tiny guests, plus an older sister and her little friend. The adults outnumbered the children who all sat on the floor around a tablecloth that was soon filled with chunks of vegetables, tiny sandwiches in dinosaur shapes, Hula Hoops and chopped up fruit.

Harry's dad, who introduced himself as Phil, offered the adults beer or wine while his wife, Fran, sorted out the children.

"Hi Hannah haven't seen you in ages. How are you?"

Hannah turned to see Nicky whom she'd met at antenatal classes and who had had her baby within days of Elizabeth's birth. Nicky had been her salvation when her first nanny had left and she'd been a good friend. She felt an immediate remorse that she hadn't seen her for months.

"Don't look like that." Nicky hugged her. Hannah winced. "Are you okay?"

"Old war wound." Hannah smiled; Nicky gave her a knowing look and was about to say something more when both of them jumped as a piercing scream filled the room. Harry had picked up a bowl of grapes and hurled it at a little girl with beautiful auburn curls called Samantha, catching the side of her head with a resounding thump. As her mother went to comfort her, it seemed to be a cue for all the other children to start crying. Except for Elizabeth who stood in front of her mother, wagging a finger.

"Naughty boy."

Hannah had to stifle a laugh and hugged Elizabeth. After what seemed a long and noisy interim, order and peace were restored and a game of pass the parcel distracted the tearful guests. Fran was doing an amazing job making sure each child got a turn to unwrap a layer of paper and find a prize when the music stopped.

Hannah turned to Nicky. "How are you?" She noticed the orange juice.

"Pregnant." She beamed at Hannah. "Five months."

"Congratulations." For a moment Hannah remembered her own second pregnancy and how that had ended in a miscarriage. A metaphor for her relationship with Tom.

"To be honest," Nicky was saying, "that's why I haven't been in touch. Morning sickness was horrendous this time. Couldn't keep a thing down all day. But I have been keeping track of your exploits."

"Really?" Hannah was saved from any other comment as Fran brought in a cake in the shape of Thomas the Tank Engine and everyone joined in a resounding chorus of *Happy Birthday*.

Phil came over to top up her glass. "Come into the kitchen, there's someone who wants to say hello."

Hannah made an apologetic face at Nicky and followed their host out of the room. She didn't even get to the kitchen before a flashbulb blinded her. She heard someone say "thanks mate," before he pushed past them and left.

Phil had disappeared back into the sitting room with his bottle of wine. She was furious but it was all over so quickly she felt she could almost have imagined it. There was little purpose in making a scene. However she'd make a point of finding out more about Phil. What a shitty thing to do. She sighed and tried to be charitable. Maybe they were just hard up and were happy to make some easy cash? But why on earth would anyone want a photo of her at a children's party?

Hannah was relieved to see that the party was breaking up. Her chance to get out of the house and think. She picked up Elizabeth, said a hurried goodbye and left. She was angry, especially as the incident had followed the note about someone taking photos of her from a house opposite hers. Why anyone would want a photo of her like that? Unless they were trying to intimidate her. It would take more than that amateur attempt. She metaphorically girded her loins and listened to Elizabeth chatting to herself about the party. As they arrived home, Hannah saw someone had left a parcel on the doorstep and just managed to pull her daughter away from touching it.

Shaking she found her mobile in her bag and pressed the number she'd been given for emergencies hoping she wasn't overreacting.

Within minutes a car arrived; they got in and sped away.

"I HOPE YOU didn't mind us turning up here unannounced like this, Celia." Hannah had alerted Lady Rayman that they were on their way in the car.

"Mind? I'd have been offended if you hadn't. Mary and I hope you'll always feel welcome here. Whatever the circumstances."

Mary had taken the sleepy Elizabeth off for a bath. "Is there anything else you need?"

"No, thanks to your foresight, I have everything we need." It had been Celia's suggestion some time ago that Hannah should always have an 'escape route'—a safe house in their home as her own parents were in France. Hannah had assumed she would never need it. Now she was grateful for Celia's prescience.

Celia looked thoughtful. "How are you getting on with Leo?"

"Leo?" Hannah was thrown off guard by the change of subject.

"Yes, Joan's son." Celia smiled. "Rumour had it at the funeral that you were helping him and... well, he's a very attractive man. And single, too."

"Celia! Don't you think he's gay?" It wasn't really a question.

"I can't say I've given his sexuality much thought. But he was married and has those two lovely girls."

Hannah found it hard to believe that after what Celia and Mary had been through she could be so blinkered. Then she admonished herself. What made her an expert on human sexuality just because she had a couple of gay friends? It crossed her mind that she'd hoped Leo was gay to avoid any possible complications. Even Claudia had commented about her missing opportunities, and she didn't think the DI was particularly attuned to romantic undercurrents. Claudia seemed to be immune to any romantic entanglements herself.

Hannah's phone rang. The person at the other end assured her that the box left on her doorstep had been a false alarm. Hannah felt silly for overreacting. But maybe not. The box had been empty. A joke or more intimidation? But why? And who was behind such puerile pranks? Were they just testing her reaction? A toe in the water? Or maybe someone had wanted her to be away from her house. These thoughts circled in her mind and sickened her.

Hannah was glad of Celia and Mary's company for the evening and the lunch they had already invited her to the following day. Elizabeth was in her element, charming Celia and Mary and lapping up all the attention. They were two surrogate doting grannies that indulged the little girl and made Hannah feel more relaxed than she'd felt for a while. She'd even managed to laugh when she regaled then with the tale of the photographer at Harry's party.

Eventually it was time to return home. Elizabeth was exhausted and cranky by then, but Hannah was in a much better frame of mind. Once her daughter was in bed, Hannah checked her emails. Only one and that was from Rory, who hadn't been able to find out anything about photos being taken of her house. Not press then, she thought. Rory's information was always good. But if not press, who was behind the surveillance?

SIXTEEN

DI MIKE BENTON eventually got back to Hannah on Monday morning. He had arranged for someone to check out number five and also to speak to Hazel, who lived next door but one. It transpired, after some probing, that Hazel had actually been given some money to write that note and pop it through Hannah's door.

"Really? What on earth for?" Hannah felt saddened.

"Maybe they wanted to spook you or get a reaction. The place is empty now. Hazel gave us a description, but to be honest it could have been anyone."

"But it's all so petty." She told him about the incident at the birthday party, and the empty box left on her doorstep. Mike was aware of the special numbers Hannah had for protection.

"Good grief what's wrong with these people." Hannah could hear the DI tapping his pen in irritation. "Difficult to see what they hope to achieve, whoever they are. Try not to let it get to you."

Easier said than done, thought Hannah as she looked at the list she'd made of people to try and see regarding Joan Ballantyne.

The first one, she thought, should be Diana Stowbridge. The actress would be expecting her call. However she sounded flustered when Hannah rang.

"Oh Hannah, how lovely to hear from you! Listen I'm rather busy at the moment. Could I call you back? Probably tomorrow?"

"Of course." Hannah gave her number, irritated that Diana, who had been so keen to talk with her, was now unavailable.

She went back to her list: Charlie Steeley, the assistant stage manager at the theatre. Probably someone who had his finger on the pulse and knew all the backstage gossip. Hannah looked at his photo. He looked to be in his twenties. Dark curly hair, five o'clock shadow. Nice suit. Medium height and build. He looked devastated. As though this had been his first funeral. Maybe it was. Hannah rang the number he had given to Edith.

He answered on the second ring. "Charlie Steeley."

Hannah took a deep breath. "Hello Mr Steeley. My name's Hannah Weybridge and you may have heard that I am Joan Ballantyne's official biographer."

There was a slight pause. "Oh yes, I think I saw you at the funeral with Sir David Powys, our director. How can I help you?"

"I wondered if we could meet for a chat about Joan —just for some background info."

Again the pause. "I'm sure there must be others far better qualified than I." The reply seemed officious. He spoke almost as though English was not his first language.

"I'm talking to as many people as I can to get a rounded view of her."

Charlie seemed to be considering his options. "Would I be named? Quoted?"

"Only if you wanted to be."

"Okay. How long will it take? I'm due at the theatre at five, so some time before then would be okay."

They agreed to meet at a café near The Old Vic theatre at four and Charlie rang off.

Hannah was loath to contact Sir David Powys, the director, after his attitude towards her at the funeral. She had been hoping that Diana Stowbridge would smooth the way for her. She looked at the photos Edith had taken of him. He looked as though he'd been charming to everyone except her. But then she saw another photo, taken from a different angle, of Sir David talking with her. He was smiling. Not the expression she remembered. Could she have been mistaken? Then she realised she wasn't looking at him in the photo…her attention was focused on someone she couldn't see.

Her phone rang and she answered automatically.

"Hello, this is Sir David Powys' PA. He was wondering if we could set up a meeting. Today if possible?" Her voice sounded calm and reassuring, but her tone suggested she was not expecting a negative response.

The decision had been taken out of Hannah's hands and she agreed to meet the director at the theatre where he had an office.

HANNAH LEAFED THROUGH the notes she'd made from her interviews with Joan Ballantyne. She'd mentioned the director several times—mostly complimentary. Hannah giggled at the theatrical leading lady's description of him as a "dear boy". She had time to skim the press cuttings she called in so that she had a fairly rudimentary knowledge of his career, and the little of his private life he gave away. It intrigued her that he had taken the initiative to arrange the meeting, but maybe he just wanted to get the interview over and done with. She'd soon find out.

As she had plenty of time, Hannah decided to take the bus to Waterloo. She wanted to be out in the company of other people, albeit strangers. She packed her briefcase, pinned on her lapel camera and was ready to go. As she set the alarm, she acknowledged to herself how quiet the house was and how much she missed listening to Janet and Elizabeth chatting and playing together. She locked the door and looked over to number 5. No sign of anyone curtain twitching. In fact the road was suspiciously quiet and empty. She hardly knew her neighbours, and she missed having coffee and cake with Leah at number 9, who was now engrossed in her new charity work. Hannah realised how selfish she was being. She walked past Hazel Smith's house, which had been divided into two flats and wondered why her neighbour had written that note for the 'spy' as she thought of the hidden photographer. Was he the same one who paid Phil at his son Harry's party? And if so why? A picture of her in a domestic scene was hardly newsworthy. Maybe it was just as Mike had said. Someone was trying to spook her. Sod them all.

As she walked down North Cross Road, she heard her name called and turned to see Nicky waving at her. She stopped and waited for her to cross the road. "Hi. Glad I've seen you. I was going to ring but—" she caught her breath. "Sorry a bit breathless at the moment. Anyway what was all that about at Harry's birthday party? Fran was furious with Phil, and they were having a right humdinger in front of everyone who was left there. Apparently he took a backhander from that bloke so he could get a photo of you. What a piece of work. Are you okay?"

Hannah smiled at her. If she'd been so worried, why hadn't she phoned that evening? But then the world did not revolve around her. "I'm fine and I'm on my way to interview someone so I can't stop."

"Right. Well, let's get together soon."

Hannah was going to make a sharp reply, but remembered in time that she didn't exactly have many friends and Nicky had been good to her in the past. "We will. Promise."

THE 176 ARRIVED at the bus stop in front of the Post Office in Lordship Lane a few minutes after Hannah. There was plenty of space and she took a window seat behind two well-dressed women who looked as though they were off for some retail therapy. They chatted non-stop and Hannah let the ebb and flow of their conversation wash over her as she stared out of the window thinking about the interview ahead. Sir David was right about one thing, she thought, writing biographies was a new departure for her and she wasn't at all sure it was a happy one or one that fitted her skills such as they were. Then she remembered he had referred to her injury. She had checked over the cuttings relating to the arrest of Edward Peters at Heathrow. *The News* stated that their journalist had been injured. No more. No sensationalism. And really Sir David hadn't implied in depth knowledge of her. She was being paranoid.

The bus had a change of drivers at Camberwell, but the two women in front of her didn't seem bothered as they continued their conversation, which filtered up to Hannah.

"But why would she kill herself? Just when everything was going so well for her and her career?"

"Who knows? Do you remember when we saw her in that weird production of Anthony and Cleopatra?"

Hannah opened her briefcase and switched on her Dictaphone and leaned forward a little.

"Wasn't she pregnant then?"

"That was the rumour when she fainted on stage one night." The woman passed her friend a packet of mints.

"No thanks. But she never had a baby?"

"How do you know?"

"There's only the one son, that gorgeous actor Leo Hawkins. No mention of any other."

"That doesn't mean there wasn't one." The woman stood to ring the bell and both women alighted.

As the bus moved off, Hannah got a good look at them and took a couple of photos. Silly she knew. She was unlikely to bump into them again, but it gave her a sense of being in control. With a start, she realised she'd reached her destination and quickly got off the bus. She didn't feel in the slightest in control of the imminent interview with Sir David.

SEVENTEEN

HANNAH RANG THE bell at the stage door; it was immediately answered by a man who appeared to be in his late forties. His long sandy hair teased the collar of his plaid shirt, which he wore unbuttoned over a dark brown T-shirt. He looked relaxed but ready for action. Hannah imaged he was useful in crowd control—and for gossip.

"Ms Weybridge?"

"Yes, Hannah—it's Jim, isn't it? I remember you from Joan Ballantyne's wake." Her smile worked no magic.

"Well, there's a surprise." Hannah had the feeling he had the measure of journalists and was not impressed. "Sir David is expecting you. Follow the corridor straight ahead and his PA will be waiting for you." He returned to his seat in the cubbyhole and buzzed through to the PA. A quick glance revealed a bank of pigeonholes on the wall behind him, plus a kettle and mug on a small table to one side near a miniature fridge.

"Thank you." Hannah did as instructed, and was met by the PA, who led her into an office that looked like the organised chaos of someone who was moving in—or out.

"Good afternoon, Hannah. You don't mind me calling you by your first name?"

Hannah willed herself to relax. Smile she instructed herself. Smile. "Not at all, Sir David."

"Oh, for goodness sake, call me David. Now would you like tea? Coffee?"

"Coffee please." He looked far friendlier than he had been at Joan's wake and, dressed in jeans and a jumper over an open necked shirt, far more approachable.

"Thanks Trudy," the director said to his PA, who had remained in the doorway.

"Now, if you'd like to come over here, I have the set designer's model I thought you might like to see." Hannah was intrigued; she had not expected him to be so helpful.

The set looked like an incredibly expensive dolls house. The detail was amazing right down to the props and sized-down characters. The armchair in which Joan Ballantyne's lifeless body had been discovered was empty and facing the audience as it should have been that night.

"Do these go into a museum afterwards?"

Sir David stared at her. "Do you know, I've never thought about what happens to them. I assumed the designers kept them." He laughed. "But they'd soon be overrun with them. Now come over here."

He led the way to a large table and rolled out a sheet of paper, which looked like a scaled diagram of the theatre. Plus another sheet that appeared to be the original set designs. "Here is where everyone was standing when Joan's body was discovered. Coral and Roger had just entered stage left here and Charlie, the ASM was in the wings opposite. The armchair was facing the wrong way and Roger moved it the right way, only to discover poor Joan's body after the smoke dispersed."

"The smoke?"

"Yes some device was set off when the chair moved, adding to the drama of the moment. A simple thing to effect." He turned towards the window and took a deep breath before facing Hannah again. "Now this is where everyone else in the cast and crew are. I've marked all the spots. I'm up here with sound, lighting is there… three other cast members were backstage, here. Hair and make-up were in their respective rooms here and here. The chippie had gone out for a smoke…"

"Why are you showing me all this?"

He stared at her for a moment as though he hadn't understood her question. "I thought you would be looking into her death, why she died?"

"Why would you think that?"

Trudy came in with a tray of coffee and a plate of cakes, which she put on another smaller table, and left without saying a word.

"Something to do with your reputation preceding you? Shall we?" He indicated the chairs by the coffee table. His smile reached his eyes. He looked friendly and genuinely interested.

"But I don't understand. When we met at the funeral, you were…"

"Rude. I know, and for that I apologise. But one never knows who's listening and there were people there I wouldn't want to cross."

Hannah was intrigued. "Because?"

"Some of our backers are not from the sort of financial institutions you might imagine. We rely, of course, on our theatrical angels but some of them—well put it this way they're not your usual arts supporters. Some have more dubious backgrounds."

Hannah almost choked on her coffee. "You mean they invest their ill-gotten gains…"

"Precisely." Sir David finished his coffee and poured some more for both of them. "Plus they like to push their own paths. We have one young male actor—not bad as it happens—whose family has links with the Croxtons."

Hannah must have looked at him blankly. "They ran most of Soho at one time, but they've managed to distance themselves from the strip joints and gambling dens and are now into legitimate investing. In the theatre."

"And does Joan Ballantyne's death have any connection to this?"

"I have no idea. However Joan was close to one of the Croxtons some years ago. There were all sorts of rumours flying around and then, just as suddenly, they all stopped and Joan married Patrick James."

Hannah finished her coffee. "But that was all years ago…"

"True, but revenge is a dish best served when it has cooled sufficiently that the act which inspired it has faded from memory. And, of course, sometimes you get rid of one play to promote another… for tax reasons." He sipped his coffee.

Hannah failed to follow his thought process and changed tack.

"Was there anything unusual about Joan on that day?"

Sir David considered the question. "No. We had a full house for the matinée and Joan was on top form. The play and its success brought out a new radiance in her. As far as I know she stayed in her dressing room between shows. I think Charlie, the ASM, may have popped out to buy her a sandwich, and she usually had some herbal tea concoction." He paused. "Would you like to see her dressing room?" Sir David looked relieved when she agreed, as though he wanted to be moving rather than sitting talking.

Hannah was fascinated by the warren of dark corridors backstage made narrow by rails of costumes and all sorts of props stacked in corners.

They reached the door, which bore Joan's name. "Jessica, Joan's understudy, won't use the room and I thought it best to keep it locked." He didn't explain why, but produced a key from a pocket in his jeans and went to unlock the door.

"That's strange."

"What is?"

"The door's already unlocked." He pushed open the door and stepped inside.

Hannah was expecting to see the room ransacked. But it wasn't. It had been left far tidier than Joan Ballantyne had left her bedroom at home.

Sir David glanced around. "A bit too tidy don't you think?"

"I expect the police searched the room?"

"Yes, they took her clothes, make-up, the remains of her lunch. You name it. They left it in quite a mess and told us not to touch anything as they may need to return. It wasn't exactly a crime scene but... Anyway they didn't come back. Afterwards I think Charlie must have cleaned up the room."

He walked over to the table in front of the large make-up mirror and picked up a photo-frame. The photo of a young man at his graduation had been turned upside down. Hannah felt a shiver of apprehension. Was this Charlie's handiwork? Or someone else? She took a photograph. "May I take that?"

She produced a freezer bag from her briefcase—something she'd now taken to carrying with her.

Sir David hesitated. "I'm not sure I have the authority..."

"I'd be happy to check with Leo." She brought out her mobile phone.

He smiled sadly and handed her the picture-frame. There didn't seem to be anything more to say. As Sir David accompanied her to the stage door, Hannah asked, "Is there another way out?"

"Yes we have an entry for large deliveries—like scenery—but that is rarely open. Otherwise you would have to leave via the front of house entrance or the basement bar. The bar was open between shows." He paused. "Would you like to see the show from the wings? Experience what it's like on the other side of the lights?" He smiled encouragingly.

"Yes I would."

"Good. Could you make tomorrow?" She nodded. "I'll sort that for you." He shook her hand. "And do call me if I can help with anything else. I'm looking forward to reading the finished book."

Hannah was thrown for the moment then realised he was speaking for the benefit of the stage doorman. "And thank you for agreeing to write the foreword."

"Jim, Ms Weybridge will be returning tomorrow to watch the show from the wings."

"Right you are, Sir David." Jim's smile was slightly warmer this time, but he gave her a curious look as though assessing her. She wondered if she passed muster as she left the theatre, blinked in the sunshine and made her way to her meeting with Charlie Steely.

THE ASM WAS already in the café when she arrived. He looked preoccupied, worried and didn't respond to her smile as she approached him. "Can I get you another tea or coffee? A cake?"

"Tea please, and one of those strawberry tarts would be lovely." She bought one for herself and carried the tray over to the table in the window. From where he was sitting, Charlie could see the theatre, as though he were keeping watch. Maybe keeping guard, she thought.

Hannah smiled. He avoided making eye contact. "There's nothing to worry about, Charlie. I won't quote you on anything unless you want me to. I just want some background information and thought you'd be best placed to help me."

Charlie blew on his tea. "I don't see why?" He sounded churlish. Maybe the strawberry tart would sweeten his mood.

"I thought with your job you'd be the eyes and ears of the theatre." Flattery held no sway and she couldn't read much into his answering grunt.

"How well did you know Joan Ballantyne?"

He stared out of the window. "She was very gracious. Very kind to me. Not like some."

Hannah bit into her tart and waited.

"I know an ASM isn't high up the pecking order, but some actors treat you like dirt. She never did. Such a lady. I still can't believe she's gone." He blinked away a tear.

"Sounds like she wouldn't have any enemies then."

"Why would you say that?" He stared at her, and Hannah couldn't decide whether he was cross or upset.

"Did she?"

"What?" He bit into his tart.

"Have any enemies?"

He chewed for a few moments increasing Hannah's irritation. "Don't we all? Lots of actors were jealous of her."

"Really? Why would you say that?" He shrugged, concentrating on his tart. "Do you mean other actors not in the play?"

"I don't know, it was just a thought."

It was obvious she wasn't going to get much out of Charlie so tried a different tack. "How long has Sam Smith been working at the theatre?"

"Why d'you want to know about that creep?" Hannah was stunned that Sam, who had been so kind to her in the past and had been Tom's snout at one time, should be regarded as a 'creep'.

"He's a friend of a friend of mine."

"Sorry." It was obvious Charlie didn't believe her. "He hasn't been with us long. A few weeks. He does odd jobs backstage. Runs errands—a gofer if you like."

"But you don't like him? Why?"

Charlie wiped his mouth with a paper napkin and took a swig of his tea. He checked his watch. "He seems to be nosing around a lot. I wondered if he was trying to sniff out stories for the press."

"Interesting thought." Hannah finished her tart and sat back. "But if so, Sam doesn't seem to have been successful. I haven't seen any gossip items relating to the show."

Charlie stared out of the window, his eyes on the theatre. "I can see you need to get off." She handed him her card. "If you think of anything that might be useful, do give me a call." She smiled. "And good luck." She stood up and offered her hand.

The confusion reflected in his expression made her wonder if she should have pushed him harder. But too late now. She'd give Sam a ring and see what he had to offer.

HANNAH HAILED A black cab cruising past and settled back into the seat. She fought the temptation to take out the stage set plans Sir David had given her and instead thought over the two conversations she'd had. Sir David had been charm personified and Charlie had been obstructive. She wondered why. And she hadn't asked anything about Charlie's background. An aspiring actor presumably? Was he the young man Sir David had alluded to?

Her phone rang. It was strange having all her calls diverted to this new mobile and meant she was often interrupted by a caller that would have left a message on her answerphone. This phone did take messages, but she answered anyway.

"Hello love, it's Sam Smith here."

"Sam—I was going to contact you."

"Thought you might be so saved you the bother. Saw you at Joan's wake but kept out of your way, as I didn't want to draw attention to myself."

"Oh?" Hannah was intrigued.

"Well 'ow would I know a famous journalist?" He laughed.

"Famous is stretching it a bit, Sam. I didn't see you at the wake but I did see your name and photograph. Must say I was surprised."

"Fancied a change, didn't I." It was a statement not a question. "Anyway, I've heard you're talking to everyone at the theatre and wanted to ask you not to say anything about knowing me."

Hannah hesitated. Should she tell him it was too late or hope Charlie didn't say anything? She opted for the truth—she owed him that courtesy. "Sorry Sam, I've already mentioned knowing you to Charlie. Well I said you were a friend of a friend."

Hannah thought she could hear Sam tapping the phone. Frustration or anger?

"Oh well don't suppose there's any harm done."

"How's Marti?"

There was a pause. Too long. "She's fine. Gotta go and see you soon." He hung up before she could ask anything more.

EIGHTEEN

HANNAH HAD GONE over and over the question uppermost in her mind. Who would want to get rid of Joan Ballantyne? No one seemed to think she'd taken her own life so who would benefit from her demise? So far she had been concentrating on the theatre, as that was where it had happened. She thought about those she'd already spoken to, purporting to be researching the biography. She didn't want to alarm anyone. Her brief conversation with Coral Moore and Roger Priest who had been on stage for the grim discovery had revealed little. You'd have to be an amazing actor to feign the sort of reaction that had been reported. And she hadn't yet spoken to the other members of the cast: Adrian Brown, Mark Webster and Gwen Owens. However judging by their comments to Edith, they were as mystified by Joan's demise as anyone.

Maybe the understudy? She's seen enough films where the understudy managed to scupper the star's health or caused an accident so the part went to them and they'd given a magnificent performance. She made a call to organise her next interview.

SHE'D ARRANGED TO meet Jessica Jewel, Joan's understudy, in Peckham Park, as the actress lived on the other side of the Rye in Nunhead. Hannah loved the autumnal hues the trees proudly wore, especially the golden yellow of the ginko tree. The idea of shedding the old but always with the promise of spring to come was appealing. If only... she thought. There were a few people by the pond where they had agreed to meet but she had no problem recognising Jessica as she walked towards her. She looked terrified. Why?

"Hannah?" She smiled tentatively.

"Hello Jessica. Thank you for agreeing to speak with me."

"Three line whip."

"I'm sorry?" They had sat on one of the benches.

"We were all told in no uncertain terms, by our esteemed director, to answer any questions you may have about Joan's death."

"Really? I hope I haven't inconvenienced you." Hannah's tone must have betrayed her irritation.

Jessica's smile showed Hannah why she had been chosen as Joan's understudy. There was a similarity and a sense of fun that she had noticed in the photographic portrait of Joan in the apartment.

"Not at all, but I haven't anything to say really—certainly no more than anyone else you've spoken to, I suppose."

Hannah considered this and decided on the direct and personal approach. "Why did you refuse to occupy Joan's dressing room?"

Jessica was silent for a moment, staring at two moorhens bickering over some bread. "Bad luck," she said at last looking close to tears. "Don't get me wrong. I really wanted this part. But not like this. I admired Joan. We'd been in some other shows together and a couple of films. I would never have wished her dead."

"Do you think she killed herself?"

There was a slight pause. "No. Why would she? This part was everything she wanted. And she was brilliant in it. Everyone thought so. She fed off the approbation. You should have seen her when she came off stage. She was glowing—on a complete high."

For a moment Jessica's expression looked so sad, Hannah thought she would break down in tears. However the actress rallied. "What could possibly have happened between the matinée and the evening show to make her take her own life?"

Hannah had heard all this before. "Does anyone at the theatre think she took her own life?"

Jessica shook her head and sighed. "No one admits to thinking it." Her hands dug deeply into her coat pockets. Hannah looked at the boots she was wearing and remembered what Janet had said about Joan's shoes being on the wrong feet. "When you are playing Lady Heston, do you wear the same shoes as Joan did?"

Jessica looked aghast. "Goodness no! I couldn't have…" she let the sentence hang between them. "Anyway we have—had— different sized feet. Joan moaned that the shoes pinched her toes. She was always slipping them off when she could."

"I imagine most women have had that experience. Tell me, is there any reason why Joan would have come on stage between shows?"

Jessica considered the question. "She was always very particular about props and everything being placed exactly where they should be on stage. Maybe she'd come to check on something?"

And met her killer? It was a question Hannah didn't articulate. If her killer—if she was murdered—knew her rituals, it would suggest someone close to her. Or someone who had been given that information. An inside job.

"Why didn't you want to take over Joan's dressing room?" The repetition of the question, seeming to come from nowhere, startled Jessica. She stared at her, eyes wide.

"I couldn't... I just couldn't..."

"It's only a room. It's not as if she died there and you're happy to tread the boards where she did die."

"I'm not."

"Not what."

"I'm not happy to be taking over Joan's role. I thought they'd get someone else in. Another big name. I never thought they'd use me."

"But you were her understudy, surely playing the role is part of the job description?"

Jessica's smile was sad. "You'd think so. But do you know how many understudies actually get to play the part? Hardly any. A one-off here and there if the lead has a headache or sore throat but when the show depends on a big name..."

"And this show needed Joan's name?" Hannah was doubtful. It wasn't the impression she'd been given by Sir David. Or was it?

"You'd think so. That was certainly the impression Sir David gave when we opened. However, he insisted I took over the part. Even mentioned breach of contract if I didn't take it." Jessica looked tearful. "Threatened me that I'd never work again." She sniffed. "I shouldn't be telling you all this. Please don't publish anything I've said."

"Of course not. But what about the dressing room? Why won't you use it?"

For a moment she looked both terrified and embarrassed. Her eyes widened and Hannah could hear her breath quicken. There seemed to be a sigh, a whisper that swirled around them. Hannah shivered as she heard the reply, "It's haunted."

IT WAS A tight turnaround: to collect Elizabeth from nursery and get her fed and ready for bed. Alesha was going to babysit early so Hannah could go to The Old Vic to see the performance of *Lady Heston Regrets* from backstage. It would give her the opportunity to mingle and chat, she hoped, with the crew. Alesha was on time, as usual, but it was the first time she was going to put Elizabeth to bed. Hannah tried not to betray her concern. She had written down the bedtime routine along with possible problems and what to do in those circumstances.

Aleysha read the sheet of paper and smiled broadly. "You can trust me, you know. I have looked after my little cousins."

"Oh I know. I'm just a bit on edge, that's all. Silly mummy," she said to her daughter who seemed to agree. She picked up a book and climbed onto Alesha's lap. Hannah smiled at Elizabeth's "Read 'Lesha," as there was a ring on the doorbell indicating her car had arrived.

MERCIFULLY THE TRAFFIC towards the Elephant and Castle flowed freely so she arrived at The Old Vic in a relatively relaxed state. Jim let her in at the stage door and buzzed for Charlie. "Sir David asked him to look after you this evening, Miss." He paused. "You know Joan would never have killed herself. She was having too much fun here. Enjoying life. Maybe you could find out what really happened?"

Hannah looked at him blankly. "I read *The News*. You've done some good stuff." He coughed loudly, an indication that Charlie had arrived. "Enjoy the show, Miss."

The ASM didn't look exactly pleased to see her, and Hannah could feel the animosity emanating from him as he escorted her down the corridors and finally to a chair set back from the wings—opposite where Coral and Roger would enter. Hannah smiled and thanked him.

Charlie nodded. Then said so quietly that she had to lean towards him to hear. "The creep's not in tonight." Hannah was about to answer when curtain rose on the stage. The armchair that Joan had died in had been replaced and was, mercifully, empty as the play began.

Seen from the wings, the play took on a surreal quality for Hannah. It was strange watching a production from this angle and she was distracted by movements and whispered conversations. She would never have imagined so much going on. A tiredness threatened to blunt her reactions, but the cast and crew, she noted, seemed nervous. A couple of times, she intercepted awkward glances in her direction.

She was intrigued when Jessica Jewell made her appearance. There seemed to be a frisson of expectation from the audience. Although younger than Joan, with the wig and make-up she looked remarkably like her predecessor. The air seemed cooler. Jessica stumbled over a line and Hannah knew exactly why. The air was filled with the scent of Chanel No 5. Joan's perfume. No one else seemed to have noticed except her and Jessica, who took a deep breath and continued her scene.

"Did you sense it?" She whispered, as she rushed past Hannah for a costume change. "Now do you believe me?"

Hannah thought back to their conversation in the park. Jessica had told her that she'd felt a blast of icy air when she'd gone into Joan's dressing room, after she'd died. It convinced her Joan did not want her there. And did not want her playing her role. Hannah didn't follow the logic of that – unless Jessica had been involved in her death in some way and that didn't seem probable.

"Why would you think that?" Hannah thought the actress was reading far too much into her experience.

"I don't know. It seems fanciful, but I keep smelling her perfume as well."

Hannah concentrated on the mallards gliding by in a group. "I smell freesia sometimes. At odd times. Often at night. But I always find it reassuring. As though someone is sending a hug you can't see or feel."

Jessica stared at her. "Well, I don't feel comforted. I feel freaked out."

"Just supposing for one moment Joan's spirit is trying to contact you. Why would she want to scare you? Did you ever upset her?"

"No. Far from it." Jessica looked close to tears.

"Do you think she's trying to warn you?"

Jessica's eyes widened. "I've never thought of it like that. Why do you think you smell the freesia?"

Hannah felt a lump rising in her throat. "My best friend was murdered at the beginning of the year. She knew I loved freesias... Maybe it's just wishful thinking."

Back in the present, Hannah realised she'd missed a chunk of the action. She decided to leave and whispered to Charlie. There seemed little point to staying and she was aware of the undercurrent of antagonism towards her.

Charlie left her at the end of the corridor, which led to the stage door.

Jim looked up from the crossword he was doing. "Play not to your liking?"

Hannah's embarrassment was obvious. "I found watching it from that angle detracted from my enjoyment."

"Did you now?" He stared at her. "Shall I get you a taxi?"

She smiled. "Thank you but I'll get one going into the station. Tell me, Jim, have you ever heard of any hauntings here?"

He looked at her and grinned. "Find me a theatre that doesn't have a resident ghost. All part and parcel of the make-believe if you ask me. Someone been telling you otherwise?"

Hannah shook her head. "Tell you what, though. It wouldn't surprise me if Joan was still hovering. Just the sort of thing she'd do for a laugh. Don't forget what I said earlier. We're relying on you."

Hannah bade him goodnight and picked up a taxi straight away. She pondered Jim's words: "We're relying on you." Who was 'we'? Not Coral Moore and Roger Priest, if their reactions to her were anything to go by. She was dozing as the driver pulled up outside her home.

Alesha was surprised to see her back so early. "I thought you'd be back much later."

"So did I, but it wasn't a comfortable feeling backstage so I decided to give them all a break and leave. Everything go okay with Elizabeth?"

Alesha laughed and packed up her books. "Yes she was lovely. No problems at all. I'll call my dad if that's okay?"

"Of course." Hannah handed her some money.

"That's too much."

"It's what I booked you for."

Sanjay arrived to collect his daughter and, after locking up, Hannah looked in on Elizabeth, who was sleeping in peacefully and went to bed thinking about haunted theatres, but dreamed of nothing more ghostly than walking in the park with Elizabeth laughing and running ahead of her.

NINETEEN

THE NEXT MORNING, Hannah picked up her new phone absentmindedly when it rang. For second she had wondered about letting it go through to voicemail but she welcomed a distraction. She was struggling with Joan Ballantyne's narrative and she still hadn't interviewed half the people she needed to. Fortunately one of those was now at the other end of the line.

"Darling. Diana Stowbridge here. So sorry I haven't been in touch sooner but I… well, I'm here now. I wondered if you would like to come over for a chat."

Hannah only just managed to stifle a sigh of exasperation. She seemed to be at everyone's beck and call. "It would be a pleasure Diana. Where do you live?"

"Clapham." Diana gave her the address. "Do you think you could come over this afternoon? I may have to be out of town tomorrow and I don't know when I'll be back."

HANNAH PAID THE minicab driver and took stock. Diana Stowbridge lived in one of the few three storey houses in the road that hadn't been converted into flats. It had a weathered look about it, and Hannah assumed she must have lived there for some time, brought up her family there.

When she'd met Diana at the funeral she'd sounded furious about Joan's death being considered as suicide. However although she had insisted they meet, it had taken her some time to arrange it. What—or who—had stalled her? She rang the bell and the door was immediately opened by a young boy who barged straight into her as he left.

With a muttered "Sorry" he hurried down the road as Diana came into the hall to greet her. "Please excuse my grandson, Hannah. No consideration for anyone but himself. Do come in."

She took Hannah's coat and led her into what she called the drawing room. The walls were adorned with framed photos from

Diana's career on stage and screen and, of late, television. In the alcoves either side of the fireplace were bookshelves. Hannah would have loved to explore their contents but Diana indicated a chair. "Do sit down, my dear. Would you like some tea or coffee?"

"No, thank you."

Diana sat down opposite her and fiddled with her bracelets. She seemed to be wearing a lot of jewellery and a rather beautiful dress. Maybe she was going out later. For someone who wanted to see her she was remarkably reticent to talk.

"Diana when we spoke at Joan's funeral you said—" Hannah consulted her notes. "That you didn't believe Joan had killed herself and that you were determined to get to the bottom of it and that you knew I could help you."

"Yes, I did." She looked uncomfortable.

"Has anything changed since then?"

"No. Not really."

"You don't sound too sure about that." Hannah smiled at the other woman who stood up and went to the bookcase. She removed a copy of *Pride and Prejudice*, flicked it open and handed Hannah the folded sheet that had been inside.

As Hannah read the words she could feel her hackles rise. "How long have you had this?"

"It came the day after the funeral."

"I'm so sorry. Did you inform the police?"

The actress shook her head. "It said not to."

"I know but… Shall we start from the beginning? I'm here now, so tell me why Joan would never have killed herself."

Diana stood up, went over to a drinks trolley. "Would you like one?" She held up a bottle of gin.

"Yes, thank you." Hannah decided she might need some Dutch courage.

Diana made short work of pouring the drinks and sat down again after handing Hannah her glass.

"I have known Joan since we attended drama school together." This fact that Hannah already knew was followed by silence.

"With Lady Celia Rayman." Hannah prompted.

"Celia Bishop as she was then." Diana sipped her drink. "The three of us were great friends. We did everything together." She stared at the window perhaps looking back in time. "It's not true that three's a crowd, you know. A triangle brings perfect equilibrium.

And so it was for us. It was just after the war and we thought anything and everything was possible. We certainly wanted to live, to enjoy ourselves. And we did. We went into rep together. We celebrated each other's successes. And then..."

Hannah waited. She could hear the faint whirr of her dictaphone. Diana finished her drink.

"And then Celia met Lord Rayman. A lovely man." She glanced at Hannah as though assessing what she knew. "As the youngest son, he had never expected to inherit the title, but both his older brothers were killed during the war. Anyway, he courted, as we used to say, Joan, but it was soon apparent that it was Celia he had really set his sights on. They married and not long after Joan married Sidney Hawkins and I married Jim."

Hannah stared at her. "James Fentonbury?"

"The very same." She smiled. "Our marriage didn't last long, but we remained friends. As did Joan, Celia and I. We didn't see Celia that often but we kept in touch. And Joan and I met regularly until..." Her voice trailed away and Hannah watched Diana's eyes fill with tears.

"Diana, I'm sorry this must be painful for you. Tell me, did Joan only have the one child? Leo?"

"What on earth makes you ask that? Of course she only had Leo. Good grief the gossip mills must be having a field day for you to ask that." Diana sounded indignant.

Hannah thought back to the two women on the bus discussing Joan Ballantyne and the rumour of a pregnancy. But she didn't mention them. She had a far more reliable source. "Well actually Celia mentioned something about another pregnancy."

"Did she indeed? Well I know nothing about it. Anyway what relevance does that have?" She finished her gin and got up to pour another. "Top up?" Hannah had only taken a few sips from hers so refused. Diana returned to her armchair. "As I was saying, Joan and I met regularly. I saw her the weekend before her death. She was so happy with her role at The Vic. And she spoke about you."

"Did she?" Hannah was intrigued and surprised. She wouldn't have thought she rated highly in Joan's topics of conversation.

"Yes. She was amazed that you would be working with her, given your reputation for investigative journalism." Hannah snorted and Diana gave her a withering look. "She also said something like—I can't quite remember the exact words, but it was along the lines of if anyone can get to the bottom of the problem, she can."

"What on earth does that mean?"

"I've no idea; something else came up and I didn't pursue it. At the time I just thought she was being fanciful or deliberately obtuse to intrigue me. Then…"

Hannah waited. Diana got up and walked to the window. "I just know she would never end her own life. She had too much to live for."

Hannah gave her a moment. "One thing that puzzles me—how did someone get Joan to meet them on stage and why kill her there?"

Diana turned back to her. "I've thought about that. It does seem strange, unless someone was trying to make a point. Although about what I don't know. But meeting on stage between shows—that might have offered an undisturbed place. Or maybe someone got her there to discuss some action in the play…"

"And got her to drink a spiked Bloody Mary?"

"Is that how she died?" Hannah nodded. "Yes that sounds implausible, as Joan would never touch alcohol before a performance."

"Maybe she thought it was a virgin." Diana looked at her blankly. "No vodka. And that would have been tasteless anyway."

"Yes that could explain it."

"And someone must have been with her as her shoes were on the wrong feet."

The actress stared at her. "Poor Joan. But that does rather point to someone in the production. Unless…" she didn't finish her thought and stared out of the window again.

Hannah looked at her watch. It was time to leave. "And what shall we do about the letter?"

When Diana turned back to face her she looked lost and defeated. "I'll leave that decision up to you."

IN THE CAB going home, Hannah's thoughts were on an internal loop. There was something she knew, which was just out of reach, tantalising her. What was the problem? Who might know? She thought of Joan's agent, Caroline Maston, but she seemed to have a particular antipathy towards her. And why was that? And then there was the matter of the letter. She took it out of her bag and read it again:

Don't pry into matters you know nothing about—it's not good for your health. Steer clear of the cops and Hannah Weybridge.

Hannah was surprised that Diana had seen her after that. No wonder she'd delayed their meeting. Diana's reaction to the mention of Joan having another child or at least being pregnant was intriguing. Hannah didn't believe her protestation. She obviously knew more than she was letting on and was cross with Celia. How much contact did those two have?

No more time for ruminations as they had reached her home.

HANNAH CHECKED HER emails and then rang DI Benton.

"To what do I owe this pleasure, Hannah?" For once Hannah thought he wasn't being sarcastic. She told him about the letter.

"Diana Stowbridge didn't keep the envelope and I wouldn't imagine there are any fingerprints worth having. What do you think?"

"God knows. Maybe someone is trying to muddy the waters?"

"Possibly. Anyway I've done my duty and kept you informed, Inspector."

"Music to my ears, Hannah. Stay safe." And with that he rang off.

THE RING AT the doorbell, just after eight, surprised Hannah. Elizabeth was tucked up in bed and she'd been wondering whether to catch up on a programme she'd recorded or settle down with some more of Joan Ballantyne's reminiscences. She looked at the video screen then opened the door. Fran, Harry's mother, stood there brandishing a bottle of wine. She smiled hesitantly. "Peace offering?"

Hannah stood aside. "Come in."

Fran followed her into the sitting room. "Hope I'm not disturbing you. I would have rung but I wasn't sure if you'd speak to me. I don't think I would in your position." She handed Hannah the wine.

"Would you like a glass?" Hannah had liked what she'd seen of Fran the few times their paths had crossed at the nursery and she was interested to hear what she had to say about her husband and the photographer.

"Please." Fran flopped onto a sofa and smiled as Hannah left the room.

She returned with glasses and a corkscrew. While she was thus occupied, she heard Fran take a deep breath. "I'm so sorry about what happened at Harry's party."

Hannah remained silent and handed her a glass of wine. Fran took a sip. "Phil is a right prat at times and I don't know what got into him." She took a gulp of her drink. "Well I do. He liked the idea of some extra money and the thought that he'd be quoted in some newspaper article."

Hannah felt sick. "Was he?"

Fran's laugh sounded bitter. "No, what could he say? He doesn't know you. But he did get £50."

Hannah didn't know whether to feel relief or disgust. Into her mind came the thought of Judas and his thirty pieces of silver. For all the good they did him.

"Anyway I made him hand it over." She gave her host two twenties and a ten. "Thought you might put it to better use."

Hannah looked aghast. "No please—you keep it, Fran."

The other woman looked uncertain as though waging an internal battle. "Well, if you're sure. But Phil won't be getting his hands on it."

"Good. But how did the photographer even know I'd be at the party. Did he know Phil?"

Fran rolled her eyes. "Allegedly they met in the pub. Phil was sounding off about Harry's party and the nursery. Apparently this bloke knew your daughter went to Little Boots and asked if Phil knew you. The rest as they say is history. Hannah are you okay you've gone very pale?"

Hannah swallowed some wine. "Yes sorry. I'm horrified that he knows where Elizabeth goes to nursery. I…"

"Put your head between your knees." Fran was beside her, a hand on her back. After a minute or so, she eased her up. She looked confused and uncertain. "I'm so sorry we've caused you such distress."

The smile Hannah produced wavered. "It's not your fault Fran, really."

AS THE LEVEL in the wine bottle went down, their conversation moved on. Fran was funny and good company and Hannah gradually relaxed, although at the back of her mind, she wondered about the relationship between her and Phil.

"Shall I open another? If you can stay that is?"

"Oh go on—I'm only going back to one of Phil's sulks." She made a face and Hannah popped into the kitchen where, fortunately, she had a bottle in the fridge.

When she returned, Fran was studying Edith's framed photos of Elizabeth, which Hannah had placed on the mantelpiece. "These are fabulous."

Hannah filled their glasses. "They are, aren't they? A friend took them."

"Lucky you to have such talented friends."

Was she imagining a slight barb in that comment? But Fran turned round all smiles. "What do you do, Fran?"

"I make celebration cakes—among other things."

Hannah laughed. "I might have guessed seeing that Thomas the Tank Engine cake you made for Harry. I would never be able to produce such a masterpiece."

Fran fished inside her bag. "This is my card if you ever need a cake or a caterer. Mates' rates."

Hannah stared at the name. "You kept your maiden name for work then?"

"Yes—made sense as I was beginning to make a go of it." She finished her wine and glanced at the clock on the mantelpiece. "I should be going. The kids wake up early regardless of what time I go to bed. Thanks for being so understanding about Phil."

Hannah wasn't sure she had been, but she'd obviously given the right impression and saw her guest to the door. She could see Fran looking at the security locks but she made no comment, for which Hannah was grateful. But there was something that was not quite right about the visit that she couldn't put her finger on. At least she couldn't until she woke up with a start in the middle of the night. Fran Croxton—now she remembered where she knew the name from and, if she was right, it was not a good omen.

TWENTY

HANNAH MADE THE call she knew she had been putting off. James Fentonbury—in her eyes at least—was a person of interest.

"Good morning, Hannah. I was wondering when you were going to get around to me." His voice sounded just like that of the message left on her answering machine the day her obituary of Joan Ballantyne had appeared, but this time there was no hint of menace.

Hannah had thought out how she was going to approach him. "Oh you know, saving the good wine 'til last." She hoped the joke would flatter him.

He chuckled. "Yes, Diana told me you been to see her. How was she? I thought she was a bit down the last time I saw her."

"Oh when was that?"

"A few days before you. We had some business to attend to in Suffolk."

Hannah wondered what that was, but it probably had nothing to do with Joan's death—or her.

"Did you show you the threatening letter she'd received?"

"No, she didn't. I wonder why? Anyway, I assume you'd like to meet up and talk about the dearly departed Joan?"

Hannah forced herself not to react to the barb. "I would. When would suit you?"

James seemed to be considering this. "Are you free for lunch?"

The invitation took her by surprise. "What today?"

"Yes, why not. We have to eat."

"True." Hannah didn't really want to waste time travelling into town and was about to say so, when James suggested a local pub.

"I'll be in your neck of the woods later, so how about meeting at the East Dulwich Tavern? Say one o'clock?"

It was only after she had agreed and finished the call that Hannah was brought up short. How, and more to the point why, did he know where she lived? A shiver ran down her body and her scar itched. Whatever James Fentonbury was up to, at least they were meeting in a public place.

LOOKING AGAIN AT the photos from the wake, Hannah mentally ticked off those people she had spoken to and those she had dismissed as improbable perpetrators.

Motive, means and opportunity: no one seemed to have all three, although opportunity and means seemed to indicate someone connected with the theatre. But what of motive? That was the question and made her think that whoever perpetrated the crime did so for another party.

Who had Joan Ballantyne upset or offended? Or was Joan's death a threat or payback for a different reason altogether?

THURSDAY LUNCHTIME WAS relatively quiet in the pub. James was at the bar, entertaining the staff with some showbiz story or other. Lots of actors, like those in *The Bill*, lived in the area, so locals were used to seeing faces from their television screens appear in shops, pubs and restaurants. James had been in a major TV series that had recently been broadcast. In his sixties, he had aged well and had a devilish charm about him.

"Hannah. Lovely to see you." He kissed her on both cheeks. "White wine?"

Hannah could see the staff wondering who the heck she was and smiled. "Yes please."

He picked up a menu with the drinks and steered her to a table away from the window. Once they were settled, he raised his glass. "To Joan."

Hannah was perplexed. He was totally different in these surroundings. Then she chided herself. She'd only met him once before at Joan's wake. Post funeral was not a good time to judge someone.

"So, how can I help you?"

Hannah wanted to ask why he had left that message on her answerphone, but she had no actual proof the voice was his.

"Tell me about Joan. Your group must have been fun in those post war years."

He took a long draught of his beer. "We were hardly a group. The girls were, of course. The eternal triangle, for a while at least. They had their rivalries, don't get me wrong. But they were tight-knit and had each other's backs. And I knew Hawkins but Rayman was an enigma. And then he disappeared. Strange that he has never turned up anywhere."

Hannah nodded. "Perhaps he died."

"Perhaps he did. Like my marriage to the adorable Diana. Doomed as a marriage, but we've stayed friends ever since. But you're right, we did have fun after the war and in the fifties. And we've all done well in our careers. Except Celia of course. But I don't think she was ever cut out for acting. She made a different life for herself. Dreadful about her daughter."

"Yes. It was."

He looked about to continue in that vein, then caught sight of Hannah's expression and rightly thought better of it.

"What would you like to eat?" he asked, as the barman hovered by them. They both ordered a ploughman's.

"Do you think Joan killed herself?"

"No I don't."

Hannah waited for him to elaborate. "I don't think she killed herself because I think I know who murdered her."

HANNAH HAD A lot to think about. After they'd finished eating, James suggested a walk in Goose Green, just across the road from the pub. She assumed this was because he didn't want to be overheard. She was right. As they walked towards a bench, he linked arms with her. "I want you to promise me you'll be very careful who you share this with, Hannah. And I want you to be vigilant in keeping yourself safe."

Wide-eyed, she nodded, wondering if she'd just walked into a trap. The green was almost deserted; it would be easy to…

He reached into the inside pocket of his overcoat. Hannah tensed. A dog barked and jumped up at her as the owner rushed over to apologise. Hannah smiled.

"Irritating mutt," James mumbled, as he handed her an envelope. "I've written down some names of interest for you. One is Albert Croxton. Years ago he and his 'outfit' for want of a better word, ran most of the strip clubs and illegal gambling dens in Soho. And he liked to party—especially with the theatre crowd. He and his cohort got out before the vice squad managed to pin a murder on them and went legit. Croxton had enough money to invest in theatres and film companies, and to all intents and purposes, he now lives a life above reproach."

He stared into the distance. Hannah studied his profile, which resembled Michael Cushing or as she remembered him from old movies. "So what does all this have to do with Joan's death?"

"Maybe everything or nothing." His smile was tinged with sadness, regret perhaps. "He had a fling with Joan in the sixties. Maybe that was the reason she and Hawkins divorced. But nothing came of it. Albert was married and his catholic wife had no intention of giving him his freedom. Joan married Patrick James and that was that. But there were rumours."

"About a pregnancy? Another child?"

He glanced down at her. "Yes." They had reached the other side of Goose Green, in the shadow of St John The Evangelist church. The clock chimed the hour. "I can't think of anyone who would want Joan dead unless…"

By mutual consent, they had walked into the churchyard and sat on a bench dedicated to the memory of some long dead worshipper. "Unless they wanted to get back at someone else. I wonder what Albert Croxton thinks of it all?" He looked at his watch. "Better get a move on."

They stood and walked back into the Green. Hannah asked the question that had been niggling at the back of her mind.

"How did you know where I live, James?"

"Leo Hawkins mentioned it."

That came out too pat, as though he had anticipated the question. Hannah had no doubt that if she asked Leo he would probably say something along the lines of "sorry I may have mentioned your address when we were talking the other day. Hope that wasn't wrong?" But Hannah was convinced he had known before that. She remembered the phone message. He knew all about her. But from whom and why?

"And the message you left on my answerphone?"

He squeezed her arm. "You knew it was me?"

"Not at first. But I did after I heard you speak at the wake. You have a distinctive voice."

He smiled. "A blessing and a curse."

"But why an anonymous call?"

"For that I apologise. I was upset. I wanted you to dig deeper to find out what really happened."

"A straight request would have been easier."

"But what would be the fun in that? Now I must leave you. Remember what I said. Be vigilant." He kissed her lightly on both cheeks and strode off towards East Dulwich station.

Hannah stared after him. How much could she trust him? That was an imponderable question.

Hannah was eager to get home and open the envelope. When she did she was completely thrown. Albert Croxton's name was there as James had said. But this was the only name apart from the Downs Mob and the instruction to "check them out but be careful!" What was James Fentonbury playing at?

TWENTY-ONE

HANNAH WAS EXTREMELY grateful that Rory had got one of the subs to research the cast and crew of *Lady Heston Regrets*. He'd emailed over the results a while ago but she'd only glanced through them. No surprises, she thought as she flipped through the sheets she had printed out so she could highlight and make notes. Now she needed to start again, more methodically, checking dates against each other and double checking with her own notes she'd made since— and Joan's.

Something made her go back to Coral Moore and Roger Priest. They were the actors in the opening scene. According to her interview with Sir David, Roger had turned around the armchair— apparently he had more or less completed the action without thinking and then there was the puff of smoke before Joan's body was revealed. Where was he between shows? In his dressing room, or so he said. There was no way of proving or disproving. Then she remembered the stage doorman. She thought back to their conversation. He would know who had left the theatre and when they returned.

She called him and was surprised when he remarked that he'd have to get back to her on that one. Perhaps someone was in earshot. She'd noticed how discreet he'd been at the theatre.

Forty minutes later, there was a ring at her doorbell. A courier. She opened the door to be handed an envelope and signed the log.

Back at her desk, she was surprised to see a list of arrivals and departures for 28 September and a note which read: "Dear Hannah, I'd already made this list for the police, but the detective who had been here said it wasn't necessary. I kept it just in case. Take care and best wishes, Jim."

The detective was, she knew, DS Farnham who had been dismissive of Janet's observation as well. Why? Was he trying to block any investigation?

Looking down the list of comings and goings, she wasn't surprised to see that Charlie Steely, the ASM, had popped out just before curtain down and returned soon after. Presumably he had bought sandwiches for cast members who wanted to remain in their dressing rooms. Sam Smith had also gone out between shows. There were no untoward arrivals or departures. At least, not via the stage door. Another dead end.

However someone, person unknown, had managed to get Joan Ballantyne on to the stage and had presumably enticed her to drink the concoction that killed her. But who? And, more to the point, how? And why?

TWENTY-TWO

IF ANYONE HAD asked Hannah where Leo Hawkins would choose to invite her to dinner, she would not have said The Ivy. She thought his predilection would be for somewhere discreet, perhaps intimate, but then again he had suggested giving the paparazzi and the gossips a run for their money.

He was already sitting at a table when she arrived, and he stood up and kissed her on both cheeks. His smile highlighted the tiredness around his eyes, the blueness of which seemed to have dimmed, and his tan had faded somewhat. However none of this had diminished his good looks and he attracted many admiring glances from other female—and some male—diners. It had slipped her mind just how famous he was as well. It must be hard always being on show.

"You look lovely." In spite of herself, Hannah blushed. She had made an effort with her hair and make-up, and the green fitted dress she was wearing was a favourite as it hid what she considered her less attractive body features. "What would you like to drink?"

Hannah ordered a Campari soda from the waiter who was hovering nearby.

"How are you? Any news from the police?"

He looked uncomfortable. "No, nothing. But let's not talk shop. I hope you're hungry? I'm famished. I've been on set all day, with only a couple of sandwiches to keep me going."

Hannah smiled. "What's it like being a heart-throb in a long series?"

He laughed. "Not half as glamorous as it may seem. On the one hand, it's brilliant having regular work and income, but sometimes you feel trapped by it." His smile made her temperature rise.

Fortunately Hannah's drink arrived and she studied the menu. They ordered their food.

Leo looked at her appraisingly. "So tell me how did you get into investigative journalism?" He looked genuinely interested. But that, of course, could all be part of a practiced act.

"More by chance than anything. Being in the right place at the right time, I suppose. Although…" she paused.

"Although?"

She bit her lip. Hard. Concentrating on not letting her eyes well up with tears. "Do you remember Liz Rayman from when you were a child?"

Leo looked bemused. "No. I… oh you mean Lizzie? Lady Rayman's daughter? Yes of course. Our mothers were friends. I saw Celia at my mother's funeral. Briefly. I had heard about Lizzie's death."

Lizzie. How strange. "I found her," she said, in little more than a whisper.

He leaned forward and covered her hand with his. "I'm so sorry. That must have been awful."

"Yes, she was one of my closest friends. I named my daughter after her." She took a gulp of her drink and moved her hand. Their wine arrived with their first course and Hannah was glad of the interruption although her appetite had diminished. She focussed on the food, willing herself to do it justice.

"What about your daughter's father? Is he on the scene?"

Hannah stared at him. She'd assumed he'd done his homework on her, but obviously not. "No, he died earlier this year." Leo didn't need to know any more than that.

Leo looked flustered. "I apologise. I seem to be putting my foot in it left, right and centre." He concentrated on his food. Then he looked up and smiled. "I like your photographer friend, Edith."

Safer ground unless he asked her how they met. "Yes, she has a fabulous eye for detail and the unusual. The photographs she took at your mother's wake were fascinating." Now she had put her foot in it. She sipped her wine. "This is delicious, thank you."

His eyes met hers and she felt a flutter in the pit of her stomach. So much for thinking he was gay. The waiter interrupted to remove their plates and refill their glasses.

"So what do you see yourself doing in the next couple of years? More of the same?"

Hannah laughed so loudly a few people looked their way. "What is this? An interview?"

"Could be." He winked at her. "No I'm just intrigued by you. You're a curious mixture of canny career woman and innocent abroad."

"Really?" Hannah could feel her hackles rising.

Leo looked bemused. "I didn't mean for that to sound either offensive or patronising."

"It sounded both. For your information, I am far from an innocent abroad. Never underestimate me. Other people have done so, and have lived to regret it."

"Well that's put me in my place." Their main course arrived and their attention focussed on what the waiter was serving, but not before Hannah caught the amused expression of a woman sitting at the next table who had obviously heard their conversation. She looked familiar, although Hannah couldn't place her. In her fifties, very well turned-out, and dining with a young man who looked so like her he had to be her son.

Hannah and Leo ate in silence. They both reached for their wine glasses at the same time and suddenly the tension eased and they both laughed. After that they chatted about inconsequential things.

A man came over to their table and slapped Leo on the back. "Good to see you out and about my man. Sorry to hear about your mother. Rum do. Look after yourself." And with a swift and appraising glance at Hannah, he left the restaurant.

"Who was that?" Hannah asked.

"Absolutely no idea." His smile melted her defences and she felt that flutter again. Pull yourself together, she told herself. This man is used to getting his own way and his charms are practiced. However, she had to admit that it was fun to be flirted with and she decided to relax and enjoy the moment.

"Would you like a desert, madam, sir?"

Hannah had eaten her fill. "No, thank you."

"How about a brandy or port?" Leo's suggestion to prolong their time together made a refusal seem churlish.

The waiter returned with their drinks.

"I'm sorry we crossed swords, Hannah. I didn't mean to offend you in any way. I wouldn't have asked you to help me if I thought you weren't up to it."

"Your confidence in me could be misplaced. I keep drawing blanks. If your mother was killed—"

"She was. I'm convinced of that."

"Then what was the motive? Do you think it has anything to do with her memoir?"

"You tell me—I haven't read any of it."

Hannah sighed. "I've found nothing that would upset someone enough to…" realising the woman at the next table was hanging on their every word, Hannah smiled and abruptly changed the subject. "Did you enjoy playing with Liz when you were children?"

Leo looked confused for a moment before replying. "Not much. She was a bossy little madam, even though I was older. But I enjoyed her company in later years."

"Oh?" Hannah was surprised. She hadn't met all Liz's friends, but she thought she would have mentioned a famous actor. "She never mentioned you."

"Why should she? We were old friends and shared the odd meal and bottle of wine. I accompanied her to a few functions when she needed a plus one and she did the same for me." He paused, his face reflecting the sadness Hannah felt. "I was out of the country when she was killed, otherwise I would have been at her funeral. I went to see Celia and Mary when I returned but that was some time later."

Hannah hardly heard what he was saying. She was back in the nightmare that was Liz's murder followed by Father Patrick's killing and Paul… She came back to the moment to see Leo staring at her in concern.

"I'm sorry, I seem to have upset you again." He signalled to the waiter and two more brandies arrived at their table.

"No, I'm sorry. Memories have a way of surfacing when you least expect them." She sipped her drink in an attempt to quell her despair. "Thank you for a delicious meal."

"Maybe next time we'll both be more…" what he was about to say was lost amid the shouts from a diner on the other side of the restaurant, who had stood up and pushed his male companion to the floor. The manager and a couple of waiters descended on the scene. "Time to leave I think." Leo signalled to their waiter and, after paying the bill, he escorted Hannah outside.

He hailed a passing taxi. "Shame we're not going in the same direction." His eyes twinkled as he took her into his arms and kissed her. Her body moved against his, she closed her eyes and for a moment she gave herself up to the delicious sensations he aroused.

"The meter's running Guv." The driver's voice ruined the moment.

Leo smiled. "Another time." His eyes held hers, then he settled her into the cab and waved her off. His promise seemed to hang in the air.

"Isn't he the chap from *Dead Voices*? My wife loves that programme."

Hannah nodded, not wishing to pursue the discussion.

"You an actress then? Been in anything I'd 'ave seen?"

She laughed. "No, far from it."

"Shame. You'd look good in that crime series."

Hannah sat back with a smile playing on her lips, amused at the driver's assumption and musing about the evening. She wondered why Lady Rayman hadn't mentioned that Leo and Liz had kept in touch. Perhaps she didn't think it relevant. Or maybe she didn't know. There were so many things she'd found out about Liz after she had died. She wished she had their time again. But didn't everyone feel that when they lost someone close? She remembered her father's grief when his own father died. "There were so many questions I didn't ask him and now I never will," he'd said. With Liz she hadn't expected their friendship to be cut short so early and with such cruel finality.

She gazed out of the window as they drove over Waterloo Bridge, then past St John's and The Old Vic. The area taunted her and echoed her fears. Death haunted her, had become her unwanted companion. Yet in the midst of death was a blossoming friendship, if she could call it that, with Leo.

All in all, it had been a strange and disquieting evening, but at least when she got home, Alesha was quietly studying. She rang her father and a few minutes later he arrived to drive her home. Hannah was left to her confused and confusing thoughts, which followed her into her dream world.

TWENTY-THREE

LEO HAWKINS SMILED to himself as he made his way to his mother's apartment the next morning. He had enjoyed Hannah's company the evening before. Life was so strange. If his mother hadn't been killed, he probably wouldn't have met her. Or he might have done at the book launch, if there was to be one. She intrigued him and it was good to be with someone who wasn't interested in being seen with him as a career boost. He also hoped his confidence in her investigating skills was not misplaced. These thoughts buoyed his mood until his arrival at Clifton House and the thought of what lay ahead lowered his spirits.

After sorting out his mother's bedroom, Leo decided to move to the kitchen to clear out the freezer. He had thought about having his mother's cleaning woman come in, but when he'd tried to ring her the number was unavailable. Had the police managed to contact her? Maybe he should ask them. He'd had the locks changed as a precaution. Once he had removed everything he wanted to keep, he'd put the apartment on the market. Or should he let it furnished? That was a possibility. A regular income would be a liberating financial bonus.

It had been horrible going through his mother's personal items. Her perfume, Chanel No 5, still pervaded the rooms. She always wore it, like a signature. He remembered sneaking one of her scarfs into his case when he went to boarding school. Something of hers to cling to, the scent evoking a maternal embrace. For a moment, he was a small boy again, craving his mother's presence. Then the adult tears flowed. Two lonelinesses—of boy and man—converged. Unable to continue, he left the room, poured himself a drink and stepped out onto her balcony hoping the autumn sunshine would dry his eyes and calm his emotions. He stared down into the communal garden, which his mother rarely visited. But he had often sat with her on this balcony sharing a bottle of wine and insider gossip. Fragments of conversation floated in and out of his mind.

Just beyond his reach, he felt that there were answers if only he could find them.

Finishing his drink, and feeling more able to continue, Leo returned to the task he'd set himself. He dumped some items unceremoniously into a black plastic sack: her cosmetics and toiletries, her underwear. How could anyone as beautifully turned out as his mother own such tatty underwear? Not all of it. Some was obviously for best. But the rest? No son, he thought, should ever have to clear out his mother's lingerie drawer. For a woman who thought nothing of spending hundreds of pounds on a top or dress, she was astoundingly miserly it seemed, about spending money on what wasn't going to be on show. As he emptied drawers, he wondered who would have to do this when he died. His daughters? The thought made him feel physically sick. He resolved to be even tidier and more careful of his personal effects.

Thinking of Olivia and Freya, he set all his mother's jewellery aside to be packed separately and taken to his apartment. It occurred to him that his aunt, Eileen, might like some mementos as well. She had phoned to offer her help, but he had felt duty-bound to do this alone.

As he worked, he remembered the gold chain and locket Hannah had retrieved from the floor and wondered why she hadn't handed it over to the police when they came. He had forgotten about it at the time. But now the memory niggled him. He'd ask her what she'd done with it. Probably slipped her mind as well.

He wondered what to do with all of Joan's clothes. Maybe he should ask Diana? She was a close friend and may have known his mother's thoughts about such things. Women, he always supposed, talked about such things. He had never had such a discussion with any of his friends—male or female.

The kitchen was much easier to tackle. He needed to empty the freezer—the fridge he had cleared when Hannah was here. Rather than inspect what was worth keeping he decided to dump everything and had black bin bags ready. He had almost finished, and was about to discard a package when he realised it was certainly not food. He unwrapped the plastic, and then opened the jiffy bag it contained. The contents left him shell-shocked.

Clutching the bag he made his way into the sitting room and poured another drink before making a call to the one person he trusted above all others.

CHARLES TRAFFORD, HIS agent and oldest friend arrived within the hour. Between them, they made arrangements for the contents of the freezer bag, which Charles took with him when he left.

As he was leaving, he hugged Leo tightly. "I'm so sorry you've had all this to contend with. But you know you can rely on me."

"Absolutely." Leo paused by the lift door. "If anything happens to me…"

"Nothing will happen to you, Leo. Stay strong."

THE NEXT DAY, Leo was back at his mother's apartment making an inventory of what was to be moved to his home—at least for the time being—and what would be left. He'd decided to let the apartment fully furnished. He'd also need to have the place deep cleaned and decorated. Focusing on the practicalities diverted his mind from the shadow of his mother's death and the thought that someone had deliberately killed her. That thought took him back to Hannah. Would she be able to solve the mystery?

The telephone rang, dragging him back to his present task and he picked up the phone. He wondered how he should answer it. Something prompted him to say: "Joan Ballantyne's phone."

There was a silence but he heard the intake of breath. "May I speak with her?"

It was Leo's turn to be silent. "I'm sorry, who's speaking?" he said quietly.

"Is she there?"

"I'm afraid not. I'm her son, Leo. And you are?"

"Oh, God. This is really awkward. I'm her daughter."

TWENTY-FOUR

OVER THE WEEKEND, Hannah wondered if she'd hear from Leo. Part of her was desperate for him to call, while her logical self told her not to act like a besotted teenager. But in odd moments she found herself thinking back to that kiss and asking what if?

Edith called. "Thought I'd better let you know that Lucy has been moved into a care home in Wyndham Road."

"Oh? When did that happen?"

"A week or two ago apparently. She'd had a few visits from Social Services and at the last one it was decided she couldn't manage on her own. Apparently Lucy had been acquiescent only packing a few things from the flat to take with her."

Hannah considered this new information. "Well I suppose when you've been living out of a cardboard box for much of your life, possessions don't mean much. If you have any that is."

"True. Anyway I got the number for you just in case you needed to contact her." She read out the number then was silent for a moment. "How are you?"

"I'm fine." Hannah thought how wonderful it would be to discuss her feelings and what was going on in her life with a close friend. She didn't know Edith well enough for that. "No news really."

"Okay maybe we could catch up soon." Did Edith sound offended, as though she'd been given the brush off?

"That would be lovely. And thanks for letting me know about Lucy."

After that, Hannah rang the care home and found out about visiting times which seemed fairly flexible and asked if there was anything Lucy needed. That was the least she could do.

HANNAH HAD AN unspent energy, so she put Elizabeth in her buggy and went off to Dulwich Park. It was a perfect autumn day and the sun was still warm. Elizabeth couldn't wait to get out of her buggy and made her way to the play park. Hannah popped her into a toddler swing and smiled at her daughter's chuckles. This is where her energies should be directed. Not towards a hypothetical romance with a glamorous actor. Who, she reminded herself, had actually asked her to investigate his mother's death. Something else she needed to concentrate on.

Elizabeth tired of the swing and made her way to the smaller slide. Hannah followed her, aware of all the families around her. Two parents, two kids.

Just then she heard Elizabeth screech, "Jo Jo" and she was hugging Joel, Linda's son.

Dave came over. "How's Hannah the hack, then." Only Linda's husband could get away with that nomenclature. He gave her a hug. Charlotte was asleep in her buggy. "We've come out to give Linda some peace so she can get on with her marking."

Hannah smiled down at Charlotte. "She looks blissful."

"Hm. Fancy feeding the ducks?"

They made their way over to the lake where Elizabeth and Joel just about shared the scraps with the wildlife. "D'you fancy coming back for a barbecue?"

Hannah swallowed hard. It was as though Dave had tuned into her loneliness. "I'd love to. I'll pick up some wine on the way back."

Evening sorted. Introspection put on hold.

TWENTY-FIVE

"HOW ARE YOU?" They were sitting in the communal lounge. A television was on in one corner with a few residents engrossed in some daytime gardening programme. The irony wasn't lost on Hannah. At the other end of the room, several board games were in progress but there were other armchairs where the occupant was looking lost and confused.

"Alright, I s'pose. The food's good and we even get a Guinness at the weekend." Lucy's smile exposed a new set of false teeth. Her hair, also, looked clean and recently cut. However the skin on her hands was still rough and looked as though there was some eczema she had been scratching. She was wearing an ill-matched skirt and jumper and what looked like a pair of men's socks and some sandals.

Hannah handed her the yellow roses she'd brought. For a moment their gazes met, perhaps both remembering Hannah's first visit to Lucy in what had been her brother's flat. Lucy had said then that no one had ever given her flowers before and roses were her favourite. Hannah passed her a carrier bag. "They said you could do with a new dressing gown."

Lucy pulled out the garment and held it to her face. "So soft." Her eyes filled with tears. "Ta luv. You didn't have to." She sniffed loudly.

Hannah handed her some tissues. "I wanted to Lucy. I'm so sorry for what happened and…"

"He killed himself. And Harry. And those other men… He was a killer."

"But he didn't kill you, Lucy. He was damaged by what had happened to him. The life he had been exposed to and corrupted by. It wasn't your fault." But maybe it was your mother's, she thought bleakly. Lucy's mother had told the terrified thirteen year-old girl that the baby she'd given birth to was dead. She'd lied. How could a mother have been so cruel?

"Yeah, but he tried to kill you as well and none of it was your doing. I feel bad I got you mixed up in it all."

"I was already involved, Lucy."

A man in a white uniform came over. He had a huge, welcoming smile. "Would you two ladies like a cup of tea?"

"She only drinks coffee, but I'll have one." Hannah smiled at Lucy's tone; she'd obviously found her feet here.

"Coffee?" he offered and Hannah nodded.

"Yes please." She smiled as he moved away from them to a trolley bearing hot water urns and crockery. "The staff seem very nice here. How are you finding it?"

Lucy cackled. "It's like Cardboard City with a few extras." She laughed at Hannah's expression. "A couple of my old mates are here. It's clean…"

"Looks a bit clinical to me." Hannah looked round at the tiled floor and white walls with just a few prints to break the monotony.

"Easier to keep clean." The man had returned with a tray of tea, coffee and an assortment of biscuits. "But we're a friendly bunch, aren't we, Lucy?"

"You are, Noah."

"Oh you're the person I spoke to on the phone." When Hannah had rung to find out about visiting and if there was anything Lucy needed, he seemed to know her well and his tone had been warm and welcoming.

"Shall I put your flowers in water for you?" Noah offered.

Lucy nodded. "I want them in my room, mind."

"Of course. I'll take them up for you."

Hannah smiled. "Well you seem to have him at your beck and call."

Lucy selected a custard cream. "'Bout time someone was. Anyway, what's this about Joan Ballantyne killing herself? On stage of all things."

Hannah carefully replaced her mug on the tray. "What do you mean?"

"What I said. I read your thing in *The News* about her dying."

Hannah had previously wondered if Lucy could actually read— she had always asked her to read out things to her. Now Lucy produced a pair of glasses and a carefully folded newspaper cutting, which was her obituary for Joan Ballantyne. "I met her once."

"Did you see her outside the theatre?" Hannah couldn't imagine Lucy actually going to see a play.

"No, it was when I was with the sisters. She was there."

She stared at Lucy for a moment in disbelief. "In a convent? When?"

Lucy seemed lost in a reverie. "Can't remember. It was ages ago now."

"Do you remember how old you were?" For an awful moment Hannah thought Lucy was referring to the time she had given birth.

"Nah. She was on some sort of retreat, I think. You know what posh people do when they want to get away... find themselves or something."

Hannah let out a deep breath and smiled at Lucy. "You're full of surprises, Lucy. What was Joan Ballantyne like?"

The biscuit seemed more of interest than the question. Lucy chewed slowly—deliberately. "She was quiet. Frightened."

"Frightened? Why?"

"Dunno. Had her own demons, I s'pose. I thought she was beautiful."

"How long did she stay for?"

"Ten days. That was the usual. She looked happier when she left. Or I thought so. But the sisters were worried about her."

"Oh why?"

"Never found out. Secretive bunch."

Hannah's phone rang. "Excuse me, Lucy, I'd better answer this."

"You go ahead, luv." Lucy helped herself to a bourbon biscuit to pass the time.

The next words Hannah heard from Rory made her head spin and the bile rise in her throat. "Sorry to break it to you like this but wanted you to know before anyone else contacted you. Hannah— Leo Hawkins has been badly assaulted. Left for dead."

TWENTY-SIX

THE DOORBELL RANG. Looking into the video screen, Hannah saw DI Benton with a woman officer in uniform. She opened the door.

"Don't look so shocked, Hannah. Aren't you going to invite us in?" He smiled as she stood aside and followed them into her sitting room. "This is PC Kim Jones." Hannah nodded in her direction.

"Is this an official visit then?"

"I'm afraid so." He and Kim sat on one of the sofas. "I expect you've heard about the assault on Leo Hawkins."

Hannah nodded. She still couldn't believe it. She felt hollow. Noah at Lucy's care home had secured a taxi for her. He had been so solicitous she had wanted to cling to him and weep on his shoulder. "Thank you for coming to see Lucy. You made her day. So sorry it had to end like this. Will you be okay?"

She had assured him she would. But she didn't feel it. She felt torn apart inside. She wanted to scream that it just wasn't fair. But then, as she knew, life wasn't fair. It could be cruel, harsh, full of injustices. In her case it was seldom easy. She felt the bile rise in her throat as the driver took every short cut possible to make sure she got home in record time. He stopped the car outside her house and opened the door for her. He took in her pallor and looked grateful she hadn't thrown up in his cab.

"How well do you know him?" Mike Benton's question brought her back to the present.

Hannah flopped onto the other sofa. Since hearing about Leo's injuries, which had left him fighting for his life in intensive care, her thoughts had been all over the place. He had hired her to investigate his mother's death but now… She was still employed to write Joan Ballantyne's biography but… And she remembered his kiss. Most of all, the kiss. She could feel the tumult of emotion threatening to overwhelm her again.

"Hannah?"

She stared uncomprehendingly at the concerned face of Mike Benton. "Is it okay if Kim makes us some coffee?"

She forced herself back into the moment, then smiled at Kim. "Of course. Everything is out on the kitchen counter, mugs in the cupboard above." It was as though she were on autopilot.

"Right." The young woman glanced at her boss before she left them.

"Sorry Hannah, but I do have to ask you a few questions. Would you like me to phone someone to be with you?"

Hannah shook her head. She remembered the first time she had met him when she'd discovered Liz's body in the crypt at St John's in Waterloo. They had come a long way in the months since then. At least she hadn't found Leo in whatever state his assailants had left him. "How did it happen? Have you got any leads?"

Mike looked uncomfortable. "I'm sorry, I can't say at the moment."

"Oh for God's sake, I'm hardly a suspect."

He raised an eyebrow but said nothing. "Okay, okay." She raised her hands in submission. "Fire away."

Kim returned with a tray of coffees and began taking notes.

"You had dinner with him—" he looked at his notebook.

"Yes. He took me to The Ivy on Friday." She waited for a snide comment but none came. The meal seemed a lifetime ago. The promise of what it may have held a shattered dream.

"And did you go on anywhere afterwards?" Benton pushed his glasses up his nose. New glasses, she noted.

"Is that you trying to be tactful, Inspector?"

"Not my strong suit, as you know." He smiled ruefully. "Did you?"

"Sorry to disappoint, but no. I got a cab home—on my own. And before you ask, my babysitter can confirm that."

He scratched his head and ran a finger inside his collar. "So how well do you know him?"

"As you know, I'm involved in writing Joan Ballantyne's biography and I only met him after her death."

"Why?"

She looked at him blankly for a moment. Had Leo been targeted because he believed his mother had been murdered? "I don't suppose it matters if I tell you now and it may have some bearing on why he was assaulted."

Hannah had the feeling that Benton knew what she was about to say. "Go on."

"He asked me to look into his mother's death as he was convinced she wouldn't have killed herself."

"He was hiring you?" It wasn't really a question and she could almost see the sigh he was attempting to suppress.

"In a manner of speaking. That was why I was at Joan's flat with him when you were called."

He tapped his pen against his cheek. "Strange that."

"What me being there?"

"No. The way the study had been trashed. Obviously by someone who didn't know that all her important files and memorabilia had been sent to you."

"Yes. Unless they were trying to make a point. Did you find any prints on that mug and picture frame?"

"No—well yes we did but none that came up on the system. Apart from Joan Ballantyne's on the frame."

"But not on the mug?"

"No."

Hannah felt a frisson of excitement. At least she'd noticed and acted on the mug in the kitchen. "I think that mug was used by the intruder."

"It's possible." Mike finished his coffee.

"Hold on a moment, there's something else." Glad of a distraction, Hannah ran up the stairs to her study, found what she had hidden carefully behind some books, and returned. She handed the locket in the plastic bag to Mike.

"I found this open on the bedroom floor. It had had the photos ripped out by the look of things. Leo thought they were of him and his father. I must have slipped it into my bag. I completely forgot about it and only came across it the other day. I'm sorry," she ended lamely.

DI Benton looked at the bag and popped it into his pocket after writing something in his notes. "No harm done." He sipped his coffee.

Her mobile phone rang. It was Georgina. "Yes I'm with the police now. Okay. I'll confirm when we're finished."

She ended the call and saw the way Benton was looking at her. "Don't people use the landline these days?"

"This is my work phone." Her mobile rang again seconds later. It was Neville Rogers. "I'm sorry, I can't talk right now. I'll call you back." She could feel her face redden, but mercifully Mike said nothing. She assumed he'd guessed what was happening.

"So do you know why anyone would want to kill Leo Hawkins?"

"Kill him? I thought…"

"It was a serious attempt on his life, Hannah. The attack had happened in Joan Ballantyne's apartment and he'd managed to alert the concierge before passing out. His attacker or attackers had left him for dead. Have you any idea why?"

"No, I don't. I have no idea who killed his mother, either. If she was killed that is."

"And Leo never mentioned being threatened by anyone?"

"Not at all." The bland line of questioning was allowing Hannah to recover her equilibrium. "I'm sorry, I really don't know him very well."

"Nevertheless, the news must have come as a horrible shock." It was the first time Kim had spoken.

Hannah wondered idly if she knew Janet. She smiled at her. "It was. I still can't believe it really. It seems so pointless."

Benton was staring at her. "But do you have you any reason to think this is connected to his mother's death?"

"Why should I…"

"Hannah, I know you. I know you won't let Joan Ballantyne's death go."

"Apart from people trying to intimidate me—and I have no idea if that's connected to Joan Ballantyne's death or not—I have nothing much to go on. I haven't discovered a motive or even any suspects. Maybe you'll have better luck when Leo is in a fit state to talk."

Benton looked as though he didn't believe her. "However, there was something I was going to ask you? A favour."

"Go on." He'd finished his coffee and had closed his pocketbook, which he opened again.

Hannah handed him a business card. "Could you run a check on this person?"

He smiled. This wasn't the first time Hannah had asked him such a favour. "I could, but I'd need to know more."

Hannah sighed. "I was at a children's birthday party on Saturday last week and the host took a bribe and allowed some random photographer to come in and take a picture of me."

Benton looked at her curiously, but made no comment. Kim was listening wide-eyed.

"I don't know why but... anyway his wife came round to apologise. She was really nice and friendly, but something didn't ring true. And when she gave me the card... the name. It rang bells and..."

Benton put the card in his pocketbook. "I'll get back to you. And Hannah—"

"Yes?"

"Please be careful. Leo Hawkins' assault was brutal—I can't say more—so don't take any risks. At all."

She nodded and saw them to the door. Kim looked at her. "At least your security is tight."

But is it tight enough? Hannah wondered as she phoned Georgina to confirm she was ready for a car to collect her.

TWENTY-SEVEN

EVERYONE IN THE boardroom looked grim. Hannah was surprised to see both Larry Jefferson and Neville Rogers there. The latter smiled at her. "I'm here in your corner, Hannah."

"Why? Am I in a fight?"

Georgina gave her a strange look. Rory smiled at her encouragingly just as Lord Gyles came in through the door at the far end of the room. His haggard expression was new to Hannah. He looked his age, although she wasn't sure what that was and had never thought to check. He ran his hands through his mass of grey hair and sighed loudly.

"First of all, Hannah, how are you? This must have come as a horrendous shock for you." He stared at her, but in a kindly uncle sort of way. She could feel her eyes welling up and fought to remain professional.

"Thank you. Yes it was. I have been questioned by the police and…"

"Right. So how are we going to handle this? Rory I'd like you to interview Hannah as part of our coverage. Nothing salacious just linking the attack on Leo to the book she is working on."

"Do we have anything more on Joan Ballantyne's death?"

Hannah wasn't sure if the editor's question was aimed at her. She swallowed hard. "I haven't found one person who thinks it was suicide, but there also doesn't seem to be a viable motive. Why would anyone want to kill her unless—" she could feel her voice deserting her.

"Unless it was to get at someone else?" Rory finished the sentence for her. "And is Leo Hawkins's assault connected?"

"Be strange if it wasn't." Larry Jefferson joined the discussion after perusing a document on the table in front of him.

"Do we have an update on his condition?" Rory scribbled something on his pad.

"Not since he was admitted to hospital. We have someone there in case of any news."

Hannah felt the nausea rising again. It was horrible talking about Leo in this way and not knowing if he would survive.

"Right this isn't getting us very much further. Rory, use one of the side offices to interview Hannah. Let's concentrate on the break in to Joan Ballantyne's apartment and his reaction plus anything else you think is relevant, Hannah."

Neville stood up. "I'll come with you, Hannah." Georgina looked about to protest, but Lord Gyles made a subtle gesture that Hannah didn't miss.

"Do you need anything else, Larry?" The proprietor's keen gaze rested on the file the lawyer was holding.

"No, I'm sure Neville will have it all sorted." A look passed between the two men and Hannah had the feeling they had had a discussion and were in agreement as to the way forward. It reassured her, as she knew Neville was on her side.

AFTER THE INTERVIEW with Rory, which went smoothly, Hannah accepted Neville's offer of a lift home. It would give them a chance to talk privately.

"I was surprised to see you here, Neville," she said as they made their way to the underground car park. She had first met the solicitor when Elizabeth's father, Paul had been killed. He had dealt with Paul's estate and was a trustee for the fund which had been set up for her daughter.

"Larry thought it would be good for you to have me here." He smiled. "I hope you didn't mind?"

"Mind? I think it's really kind of you to be involved. Unless you're charging me by the minute?"

"Not at all." He looked hurt as he unlocked the car doors. Once inside he took her hand. "I'm always here for you as a friend, Hannah."

Her "thank you" was almost lost in the wave of emotion she threatening to overcome her.

Neville drove in silence for a while. "If you need to run anything past me please do. I won't blab to Larry Jefferson in case you think I would. And he, by the way, has a great respect for you."

Hannah blew her nose noisily. "He wasn't like that when we first met."

Neville said nothing, but she had the impression he knew all about the first contract she had with *The News* and how her story about the murdered sex workers had been spiked. Water under the bridge.

Rory had been gentle in his interview but she wondered how the assault on Leo would be portrayed in the next day's papers. Fortunately, she had only a minor role in his life. She chided herself for being so selfish.

Neville drew up outside her home. "I expect you'd like some time to yourself but I can come in if you'd like me to?"

Hannah smiled. "No, but thank you for the offer."

"Take care and be careful."

"I will and thank you for everything."

With a heavy heart, she unlocked her front door and waved goodbye. Why was life always so complicated? Everyone kept telling her to be careful, but if you didn't know who the enemy was or where they'd be coming from, careful was virtually impossible to achieve.

HANNAH COLLECTED ELIZABETH from the nursery early, and they spent some extra time playing together. A couple of times she caught her daughter staring at her in an odd way. At last she said, "Mama sad," and put her little arms around Hannah's neck and kissed her over and over again. It was all she could do not to cry. All she knew was she had to keep her daughter safe.

TWENTY-EIGHT

THE NEXT MORNING she bought all the newspapers on her way back from the nursery. There was blanket coverage of the assault on Leo. Lots of background information about the actor and his life, including one or two little snippets about herself. One tabloid even had a photo of her and Leo outside The Ivy. Fortunately she was virtually unidentifiable.

The coverage in *The News* was unsurprisingly more toned down and in depth, making tenuous links to Joan Ballantyne's death and the fact that her son was convinced she had been murdered. Hannah wasn't surprised when Celia called her. A short conversation, but Liz's mother was obviously distraught. As was Diana Stowbridge. The worst thing seemed to be that no one knew the exact details of Leo's injuries and more importantly whether he would survive them.

Hannah decided to concentrate on the Joan Ballantyne manuscript. Immersing herself in work, focusing on the written word was the only way to stop her thoughts from spiralling out of control.

A CALL FROM Claudia intrigued her. She didn't even mention the attack on Leo Hawkins, but invited her to join her at Dulwich Tandoori where they usually bought their take-aways.

"Eight okay for you? Time for a babysitter to arrive?"

"Yes that would be lovely, thank you."

As usual Alesha was more than happy to earn some cash. Hannah had become increasingly fond of the girl, the young woman she was becoming. And she was certainly right about her father. No arranged marriage for his daughter. He was absolutely determined to help her as much as he could to attain her dream of becoming a doctor. She wondered what Elizabeth would dream of becoming and hoped that not having a father wouldn't be a disadvantage. In a way, Paul being dead made life less complicated. That thought made her feel guilty, but it was true. Less to explain as her daughter grew up. And the fact that Neville was a trustee meant there was at least one good man in her life looking after her interests.

ALESHA ARRIVED ON time as always. There was an excitement about her. She was aglow.

"So tell me. What's happened?" She had a shrewd idea.

"I've had an offer to study medicine. At Cardiff."

"That's fantastic. Congratulations. I bet your parents are over the moon."

Her face clouded. "Well they were hoping I'd study in London. And I may still do... but—"

"But you'd prefer not to live at home."

"Is that awful of me?"

Hannah smiled. "Of course not. It's perfectly natural. But I expect I'll feel exactly the same as them when and if Elizabeth wants to study away from home."

Alesha shook her head, went into the dining room and spread her books on the table.

"Would you consider giving another talk at my school? For the sixth form?"

Hannah hesitated. It was strange that the request had come from her and not from Linda who had invited her the first time. But she didn't want to let Alesha down and maybe the sixth form organised some of their guest speakers.

"What's the subject?"

"The working mother."

Hannah could feel her scar itch. It seemed innocuous, but Hannah had the feeling there was more to it. She pulled on her raincoat. "I'll think about it." She saw how hurt Alesha looked and could have kicked herself. She smiled. "Okay, I've thought. Of course I will. See you later." She passed the cell phone that she'd bought ages ago for Janet. "If you need me use this. My number is keyed in." Her actual motive for the phone was if she needed to contact Aleysha.

"Okay." Alesha smiled. "Enjoy yourself, Hannah."

DULWICH TANDOORI WAS a favourite with Hannah. Since Elizabeth was born she'd relied on more take-aways so a visit to the restaurant was a treat. Nurul, the manager, smiled as he took her coat.

"Lovely to see you Mrs Weybrige. Your friend is already here."

"Thank you." Hannah smiled. She had never managed to get Nurul to call her Hannah. Or Ms.

Claudia waved to her from one of the two partitioned booths. Other tables lined both walls. She stood as Hannah joined her and kissed her cheek.

"So what's all this in aid of?"

Claudia beamed at her. "We're celebrating." Hannah was thrown. "Or I am, and I wanted to share my news with you."

Hannah had a premonition she wasn't going to like Claudia's news.

The wine arrived—Claudia had ordered a bottle of Chablis along with some poppadoms and chutneys. Nurul poured them both a glass. "I'll come back for your order in a few minutes."

They clinked glasses.

"So?"

"So I'm celebrating a promotion. It was a long application process but I'm a Detective Chief Inspector now." She grinned at Hannah. "And I owe some of that to you and your investigations."

Hannah was about to dispute that, but didn't get a chance to speak.

"It involves moving into a different department." Claudia looked at her intently. "Can't say too much at the moment, but I'm really excited."

"Congratulations." Hannah raised her glass. Why did she feel deflated?

Nurul came back to take their order.

"Two minutes." Claudia turned her attention to the menu. Hannah followed suit. They both knew the menu so well it didn't take long to make their choices and they were left to pick up their conversation.

"You don't seem that pleased for me." Claudia's eyes were especially bright. Just like Alesha, another very happy person.

"Oh I am. Of course I am. It's just…" Hannah stared at the print of the Taj Mahal on the opposite side of the restaurant. The image of Princess Diana sitting on her own in front of this iconic building came to mind. She too had felt isolated and alone.

"Just what?"

Hannah was about to say "nothing" then blurted out. "It's just I've got used to relying on you, I suppose."

Claudia put her hand over Hannah's. "I'm not leaving London. Or the area and I hope we can still meet as friends?"

The knot in Hannah's stomach slowly relaxed—a little. She smiled. "I hope so too. Will this mean more of a nine to five existence?"

"Yes and no depending on the circumstances. But it's very exciting." She topped up their glasses.

"I am pleased for you Claudia. You deserve it—whatever it is." They both laughed as their food arrived.

For a while they ate in silence, occasionally commenting on the food.

"God, I needed that." Claudia dabbed her mouth with the napkin. Then drank some wine. "Shall we order another bottle?"

Hannah nodded. "We are celebrating after all."

Claudia lifted the bottle and signalled to Nurul. He came over with the wine. "How was your food?"

"Excellent as always. We haven't finished yet just pausing."

Nurul beamed and moved away.

"So shall we confront the elephant at the table?" Claudia looked serious and sad.

"Which one? There are so many."

Claudia contemplated her over the rim of her glass. "Shall we start with what I assume to be the most recent one?"

Hannah was amused that the DI—now DCI—gave nothing away. She had the feeling she was about to be interrogated but she could play the game as well. "And which one is that, may I ask?"

"There's more than one? Touché." Claudia laughed. "I was wondering how you were feeling about what happened to Leo Hawkins. It must have come as a terrible shock. And yes I did see the pap photo of you two in a clinch outside The Ivy."

"Don't believe everything you read in those rags." Hannah sipped her wine. "Strangely, although I was shocked when I first heard, the more I thought about it, the more it made sense."

"Really? Why?"

"Well, he was convinced his mother didn't take her own life but was murdered. And now we have what seems to be a senseless, attempted murder."

Claudia nodded. "I understand Mike interviewed you."

"Yes. He's come such a long way. I remember him interviewing me after I discovered Liz's body. He was horrid."

Claudia nodded. She remembered the bollocking she'd given him over that. "You've both come a long way." She smiled and refilled their glasses.

"Have you finished ladies?" Nurul had appeared at their table.

"Yes, thank you. It was delicious. Although it's convenient to have a take-away it seems to taste so much better here."

"Thank you madam." He finished clearing the table and left the dessert menu.

"So are you investigating the attack on Leo?"

"Good lord, no! I was asking as a friend. A concerned friend."

Hannah folded her napkin. "Leo Hawkins is a very attractive man. But I don't really know him. Maybe…" She sipped her wine.

"Maybe?"

"Nothing. I'm sad, of course, and concerned. I don't even know the extent of his injuries."

Claudia contented herself with that. "Have you heard from Tom?"

Hannah gave her one of those looks Claudia had got to know so well. "Have you?"

"I have as it happens. He heard about my new role—God knows how—and congratulated me. He also gave me the impression in the email that he would be staying in Australia for the foreseeable."

"That doesn't surprise me."

"Oh?"

Hannah pleated the napkin on the table. "I have—had—the impression that there was something in his past which… Oh I don't know something which haunted him."

"Do you mean about his wife's death?"

"Yes."

"How much did he tell you?"

"Only that she had died in a car accident with his best friend. He discovered that they were in fact going off together."

"Yes that's what he told me but I always thought there was something more to it."

"Did you?" Hannah was astounded. She had taken Tom's explanation at face value.

"Probably my suspicious nature."

The two women stared at each other and it was as though a beam of understanding passed between them.

"Anyway I thought we were celebrating your promotion."

"We are. And thank you."

Nurul arrived at their table again. "Ladies may I offer you a drink on the house. Port? Brandy?"

"That's very kind of you, but no thank you. Could we have the bill?"

"Of course." He returned with the bill, which Claudia paid. She finished her wine and looked at her watch. "I'm getting a cab. Shall I drop you off?"

TWENTY-NINE

CAROLINE MASTON DIDN'T waste time on social niceties. "I need to have all Joan Ballantyne's documents delivered to my office. As soon as possible." Her voice was sharp and jarred on Hannah's nerves. "I can send a courier."

"Why?" Hannah was in no mood to be bullied.

"So that you don't have the trouble of bringing the documents yourself of course." She sounded exasperated.

"No, I mean why should I give you Joan Ballantyne's documents."

"I would have thought that was obvious. I was her agent—and still am—as it stands I have the authority over her creative output."

"But not her memoir."

"I beg your pardon, but I…"

"You will have to discuss any problems you have over this with Hallstone Books and their legal team." Hannah had the distinct impression Caroline had already done this and was trying to intimidate her into giving up the documents.

"Will I indeed?" There was a pause and Hannah thought she could hear another voice in the background. "You'll regret crossing me, Ms Weybridge." And with that the line went dead.

THE NEXT CALL was from another agent: the man who represented Leo Hawkins. And Charles Trafford was far more accommodating—and charming—than Ms Maston. After talking about Leo's hospitalisation, he came to the point. "I wonder if we could meet up, Hannah? I have something here which may interest you." He didn't elaborate.

Hannah agreed to a meeting the next morning. In the meantime she contacted the cuttings department at *The News* and asked for anything they had on both agents. Better to be prepared. A while later the cuttings were faxed over. But before that, she'd had a call from Larry Jefferson.

"I understand you may have been contacted by Caroline Maston."

Hannah didn't even bother to ask how he knew. "I have."

"Don't let her bully you. And don't hand over any of Joan Ballantyne's documents."

"I wasn't going to." Hannah didn't appreciate his hectoring tone.

"No, I didn't think you would." He paused and Hannah imagined him steepling his fingers and tapping his foot. "I have just warned her that Hallstone Books will take out an injunction against her if she tries any more of her tricks. She won't want that sort of publicity. Especially now."

"Why especially now?"

"She's had a major fall out with one of her big clients and what with Joan's demise she'll be feeling the pinch as it were."

Hannah liked the idea of Caroline Maston feeling the pinch. Very much.

THE CUTTINGS DIDN'T reveal much about Charles Trafford. He was a successful entrepreneur, often seen in the company of the rich and famous. His theatrical agency had been set up by his father, which he'd taken over on his retirement. In photos, he looked the epitome of an accomplished achiever and there was not a hint of scandal or acrimony attached to his name, as far as Hannah could see.

Caroline Maston, in spite of the number of cuttings she was named in, remained an enigma. Her agency seemed to spring from nowhere. To be more accurate, she took over a small agency when the owner died. She had apparently been working as an assistant there. There was nothing about what she had been doing before that. And why should there be? Just because Hannah didn't like her attitude, didn't mean there was anything untoward in her past. Hannah drummed her fingers on her desk and decided to go back to Joan's memorabilia.

She had looked through the photograph albums the day before. There were two sets: the personal and the professional. Hannah found both fascinating. The few from her days at the Vera Green Academy often included Celia and Diana and they always looked so young, happy and full of promise.

In one of the personal albums, Hannah found a photo of Leo and Liz playing together in a garden. Hannah stared at it until it blurred as her tears fell. Two lovely people. One dead and one fighting for his life. She felt overwhelmed by the futility of life or rather death.

THIRTY

THE NEXT MORNING she was at Charles Trafford's offices punctually. His agency in Soho was housed in a modern building, which was all steel and smoked glass, so out of keeping with the district. Charles stood as his secretary led her into the inner sanctum then returned within minutes with a tray of coffee and croissants.

"I'm very pleased to meet you Hannah. I just wish it was under different circumstances."

He squeezed Hannah's hand in his rather plump one. They sat in two armchairs angled towards each other. A coffee table between them was scattered with glossy magazines. The face of Leo Hawkins graced the cover of *Hello*. He was smiling into the camera; Hannah felt her stomach clench tightly. Her scar itched. She swallowed hard to quell her emotion.

"Yes, you must be horrified by what has happened to Leo."

"Of course. I thought you would be too. I understood..." Whatever he understood was not shared. Hannah's expression warned him not to tread that path. He changed tack. "From a professional point of view, Leo is one of my top ranking clients. But it's more than that. We were at school together. Boarding school engenders enemies and friends for life. We were friends and remain so. I was best man at his wedding and am godfather to his older daughter."

Hannah studied this man as she listened to his preamble. His face was a fleshy testament to his enjoyment of the good life and his suit was skilfully tailored to disguise the extra pounds. His hair was sandy, a good camouflage for the grey that must be there.

As he poured the coffee, his sleeve moved up his arm revealing a tiny tattoo of something Hannah couldn't quite make out. "Help yourself to milk and sugar." He added both to his own cup. "I had a visit from DI Benton yesterday. I gather you know him."

It wasn't a question. Hannah nodded.

"He said he had met Leo when he reported a break-in at his mother's apartment and you had been there."

Hannah leaned forward to replace her cup and saucer on the table. "Yes I was. I had gone there with a photographer as I'm working on a book about Joan Ballantyne."

"And Leo had asked you to investigate her death."

Hannah paused not sure how much to reveal, but the way he said it suggested Leo had discussed this with him. "Yes."

"You have acquired quite a reputation, Hannah, in a relatively short space of time." He must have been aware of her change of expression. How the air around him seemed to cool. "That is in no way a criticism. On the contrary I'm impressed—full of admiration."

Hannah's scar was making itself felt again. She wanted to scratch and scratch…

"I'm sorry, I'm being clumsy. I didn't mean to offend you. I want to engage you."

Hannah stared at him. "What?"

"I want to engage your services to help discover what happened to Leo."

Hannah paused. "Charles, I'm a journalist not a private investigator."

"But you've helped other people get to the bottom of suspicious circumstances."

"Sometimes inadvertently, or in the course of my work, yes. But …"

"Whatever your fee is …?"

Hannah stood up. "As I said I'm not a private investigator. I think you have misunderstood. I am a journalist."

Charles stood facing her, his expression unreadable. "Okay. But I do have something for you." He went over to his desk then handed her an envelope. "No strings. I met with Leo on Saturday and he phoned me on Sunday—before the attack obviously. I am not at liberty to discuss all of our conversation, but Leo had had a call from someone claiming to be Joan's daughter. He had invited her to join him at Joan's apartment and she presumably was the last person to see him before the assault." He let this information sink in. Hannah felt a shift in emotions. Something wasn't right. She was sure there wasn't a daughter unless… unless she'd been deceived and lied to.

Charles' voice brought her back to the present. "When I saw him on Saturday, he asked me to pass this on to you if anything happened to him. I thought he was being dramatic." He looked desolate. "What you do with it is up to you." His expression was sombre.

"Thank you. Are you allowed to visit Leo in hospital?"

"Not at the moment. I was there when he was admitted. He's in an induced coma after being operated on."

He shook her hand. "Please get in touch if you change your mind or if I can be of any assistance."

HANNAH HAILED A taxi and slumped back in the seat. She felt confused and exhausted. She stared at the envelope in dismay. Part of her wanted to throw it out of the window, but she knew she wouldn't be able to do that. Plus, she was intrigued that someone purporting to be Joan's daughter had contacted Leo. Or maybe she didn't know Joan had died.

She opened the envelope and began reading the letter addressed to her.

"Dear Hannah,

While I was clearing out my mother's freezer, I found several surprising items. One was a parcel containing cash, which I have asked Charles to pay into your account as payment for the work you are doing—just in case anything happens to prevent me from paying you myself. Also that way the money won't be traced to me. Please continue with your investigations, especially if anything untoward happens to me. I'm not being dramatic. I have good cause to be fearful."

She stopped reading and leaned forward to tap on the dividing glass. The driver opened it. "Yes luv?"

"Sorry could you take me to Chancery Lane instead."

They were on Waterloo Bridge. The driver continued then turned left into Stamford Street, at the end of which, he took a left on to Blackfriars Bridge, the meter marking up the fare. She turned her attention back to Leo's letter:

"My other point is, please don't give anything to my mother's agent, Caroline Maston. I have a feeling she isn't totally committed to my mother's legacy. However you can trust Charles. Implicitly. We've been friends most of our lives and he is absolutely reliable. He will help if you need it..."

The taxi arrived at the mews, which housed Neville Rogers' offices and Hannah got out and rang the bell. He wasn't expecting her, so she hoped he wouldn't mind her unannounced visit.

"SO WHAT DO you think?" Hannah had been perched nervously on a chair opposite Neville as he read the letter. He was taking his time. She was sure he'd read it more than once.

"Do you know how much he paid into your account?"

"No. I only gave him my bank details when he insisted on having them to pay me for looking into his mother's death. But I told him I'd send an invoice. I haven't, of course."

"Right phone your bank now and find out."

Neville left the room to give her some privacy. When he returned she was staring at her phone as though she'd never seen it before. She looked up at him wide-eyed.

"Ten thousand pounds. Is that legal? Can he just do that? Well obviously he has but—" she was waffling, not knowing what to say.

"As long as the money hasn't been stolen, it's perfectly legal. More intriguing is why Joan Ballantyne would have hidden that amount of money in her freezer. Any ideas?"

"She was blackmailing someone? Someone had paid her off? She was hiding it for an unknown person who was blackmailing her? Oh, I don't know."

Neville's secretary came in with a tray of coffee. She smiled at Hannah, but left without a word. Perhaps legal secretaries were trained to be discreet and not react. The lawyer poured the coffees and handed a cup to Hannah.

"Don't worry about the money for the time being. Transfer it to a savings account and don't touch it. And try not to worry. You've done nothing wrong or illegal."

Hannah wondered if that was actually true, but decided that the money was the least of her problems at the moment.

A BIT OF digging in Companies House revealed that Caroline Maston had been the company secretary of Priscilla Preston Theatrical Agency until the founder died in 1973. Caroline Maston took over soon afterwards and renamed the agency Maston Enterprises. The company returns increased year on year and Ms Maston was soon the owner of a thriving business.

Hannah wondered how an assistant became the company secretary and then the owner after the death of Priscilla Preston. She didn't think Caroline would tell her if she asked.

She phoned Rory. "I'm stuck."

"Hello to you too, Hannah. And what, may I ask are you stuck with?"

"I need to find out more about Caroline Maston, but I don't know how to go about it. How do I find out more about her without alerting her?"

Later, she emailed Larry Jefferson to find out which major client had just left the agency. The reply was by return.

"Sorry I thought you would have known. It was Diana Stowbridge."

HANNAH PHONED DIANA Stowbridge, but had to be content with leaving a message. She returned to Joan's typed notes, and marked all names with a yellow highlighter and and all dates with red.

"I was stunned to see Caroline Maston working for Priscilla. The last time I had seen her was some years before and then she was Caro Reynolds." Something was crossed out here that Hannah couldn't read. And Joan's spidery handwriting was also difficult to decipher. Diana still hadn't returned her call.

Hannah emailed the cuttings department asking for anything on Priscilla Preston and her agency, as well as anything on Caro Reynolds.

Who else could help her? Her mind ran over the list of people who had been at the theatre that night. The director, Sir David, she had already interviewed. Also Charlie Steely and Jessica Jewel. She still needed to find out why Sam Smith had had a change of jobs. Names and thoughts were whirling round. She needed someone to bounce ideas off. Janet. And Janet had been on the scene the night Joan died.

She rang her former nanny. "I don't suppose you're free tomorrow evening?"

"I am as it happens. Do you want me to look after Elizabeth?"

Hannah felt a pang of remorse that she maybe took advantage of Janet's good nature. "No, I'd like to pick your brains and bounce some ideas off you. Would you like to come to supper?"

"Mm, tough call. Can I come early enough to see Elizabeth before she goes to bed?"

"Of course. You know our routine, come whenever."

THIRTY-ONE

THE NEXT MORNING, Hannah was surprised by a courier as she returned from taking Elizabeth to nursery. It was raining and the clouds matched her mood. The courier sat on his motorbike waiting for her. "Ms Weybridge? I was told to wait and get you to sign for these."

Hannah signed his sheet. "Thank you."

Inside she took off her dripping raincoat and wet shoes in the hall, and ran upstairs to her study. The package was from the cuttings department at *The News*. She was making full use of Lord Gyles' directive that she had carte blanche to use the newspaper's services. She tore open the envelope and a few sheets emerged. They were in date order, and curbing her curiosity she read them as presented.

The first was a short item from *The Stage* announcing that the Prescilla Preston Agency had just signed Joan Ballantyne. Hannah looked at the date. It was 1950, when Joan was a young and virtually unknown actress. The following three were mentions connected to another of her clients Diana Stowbridge. Hannah assumed that as they had been to drama school together, it would have been natural to share an agent. Maybe the agency had a link with the Vera Green Academy. That would make sense. She made a note to check out the Academy.

The penultimate cutting was a short piece announcing the death of Priscilla Preston. Her demise was sudden and unexpected, but there seemed to be no suspicious circumstances. She had fallen down the stairs at home where her offices were also housed and there had been a large quantity of alcohol in her blood. A tragic accident.

The obituary painted the picture of a lonely woman who had devoted herself to her clients after failing to make it as an actress herself. Joan and Diana were quoted: "I am devastated. Priscilla was so much more than an agent. She offered love and support when needed and always put our needs before hers. Perhaps I should have been a better friend."

Diana was succinct. "Priscilla was someone you always wanted on your side—more of us should have been on hers. A great loss to the profession."

The photo, obviously taken years before, revealed a woman in her prime but, in spite of her smile, Hannah felt there was an aura of sadness about her.

Then came a quote from Caroline Maston who had found Priscilla's body when she had arrived for work. "I can never thank Priscilla enough for having the confidence in me when I had none in myself. I am honoured that she bequeathed her agency to me and will endeavour to live up to her high expectations and carry on her work."

And that was it. Priscilla had died leaving Caroline as sole beneficiary. Why? Were there no relatives at all? No one who disputed the will? Apparently not.

Hannah phoned Neville. "Can I pick your brains, Neville?"

He seemed surprised. "Of course how can I be of help?"

She explained that she wanted to check a will written by Priscilla Preston and to see if there had been a previous will.

Neville laughed. "Oh, I thought you were going to ask me something difficult. It will cost you though."

Hannah waited. "Yvonne and I would love you to come over for lunch on Sunday with Elizabeth. Our children will adore her and…"

"Yes, of course, thank you!" They ended their call. If only all her negotiations could be that simple.

Hannah had almost missed the last cutting as it had got tucked behind one of the others. It was from *The Stage*—a small news item stating "Caro Reynolds, a licensed pyro-technician had been in an accident when one of her stage effects involving a waterfall of fire had gone drastically wrong. Miss Reynolds had suffered severe burns to her hands trying to extinguish the blaze but had saved the actress, Joan Ballantyne, from any harm."

Well, that was a connection and a half—and explained the gloves Caroline Maston always wore.

JANET ARRIVED JUST as Hannah was running Elizabeth's bath. She had turned up in uniform. "Sorry, I was late and didn't want to miss seeing this little darling."

Elizabeth screeched with delight as Janet pulled off her jacket and took her in her arms. "I've missed you little one."

Elizabeth plonked a sloppy kiss on her cheek. For a moment a shaft of raw jealousy gripped Hannah. She took a deep breath. "Would you like to do bath time while I finish preparing supper?"

"Yes!" screeched her child, and Janet looked as though she'd won on the Premium Bonds. Hannah left them to it.

She had a chicken roasting in the oven along with jacket potatoes. She only had the salad to prepare and turned on the radio to stop herself from eavesdropping on what was going on upstairs.

The newsreader concluded the broadcast. "We've heard that the actor, Leo Hawkins, is still in an induced coma at St Thomas's Hospital, where he was taken after being found brutally assaulted at his mother's apartment. Joan Ballantyne died on stage at The Old Vic on 28 September. She ..."

Hannah turned off the radio. She could do without that reminder. She was just opening a bottle of wine when Janet and Elizabeth appeared in the kitchen doorway, both looking relaxed and happy. Hannah could see that Janet had needed some baby time and perhaps her little daughter needed some time away from mummy. It was a hard lesson.

"Right young lady, what do you say to Janet?"

"Thank you," was followed by Elizabeth taking Janet's face in her chubby little hands and giving her another sloppy kiss. "Night, night."

HANNAH RETURNED FROM putting Elizabeth to bed a few minutes later. Being at nursery all day tired her out, so it was just a quick story before she was asleep.

Janet smiled and handed her a glass of wine. "Anything I can do?"

Hannah raised her glass to Janet. "Cheers. And no everything is ready."

They ate in the kitchen. Hannah hadn't felt so relaxed in ages but she felt Janet was on edge or at least something was bothering her.

"Everything all right at work?" she asked, as she helped herself to more salad.

Janet paused before replying. "Yes and no. I love being back on the job but my DS is a typical male chauvinist and treats me as though I only have a few brain cells and not many of those function. It's nothing I can really call him out on but he makes little snide comments and jokes about my appearance."

Hannah was immediately annoyed on her behalf. "Surely you don't have to put up with that kind of behaviour? Can't you complain to someone?"

"Not yet. I'm holding my fire." She smiled. "I have a feeling he's up to something and if I can catch him out…"

"Good." Hannah didn't want to push her on this. "Would you like some apple pie? It's not home-made I'm afraid."

"Love some."

IN THE SITTING room after they had finished the meal, Hannah topped up their glasses. Janet appraised her. "So my brains with a limited number of functioning cells are ready to be picked and you can bounce any ideas off me."

Hannah sipped her wine. "I don't know where to begin really, but as you were at the theatre shortly after Joan Ballantyne's death…"

"Ye-es?"

"I was intrigued that you noticed her shoes had been put on the wrong feet. Her understudy told me that Joan often slipped off those shoes as they pinched her feet. So was someone with her when she died and put them on her? I've been through the list of actors and backstage crew and I just can't see a connection…"

"Do you have your list?"

"In my study."

"Mind if I have a look?"

"Not at all." Hannah left the room and returned with two sheets of paper, which she handed to Janet without comment.

Janet took out her pocketbook and leafed back several pages then compared the lists. "Do you mind if I make notes on yours?"

"Go ahead." She sipped her wine in silence.

"Right," Janet said at last. "I've also added two names." She handed the sheet back to Hannah who stared at her.

"But they weren't in the cast or crew."

Janet shrugged. "But they were there when I arrived."

THIRTY-TWO

HANNAH WONDERED WHAT to expect as she and Elizabeth made their way to have lunch with Neville and his family. He had offered to collect them, but Hannah preferred to go under her own steam—or at least by cab—to their home in Stockwell. Elizabeth dozed off in her car seat, which meant she would be on good form when they arrived. She had only met Yvonne once and that was at Paul's funeral, which had been arranged by Neville. It had been a small affair at the crematorium in Streatham and there was no wake afterwards, for which Hannah had been extremely grateful. The thought of having to make small talk about the circumstances of Paul's death, which were mainly unknown to most of the mourners, terrified her. So she had only said hello to Yvonne and her impression was hazy.

However this was the woman Paul had loved and lost when she'd married Neville. Paul had never mentioned her, but she was the reason he'd been unable to commit to Hannah—and Elizabeth. She looked at her daughter and momentarily saw the father. Her vision blurred.

THE DAY BEFORE, Dave had taken Elizabeth to the park with Joel and Charlotte so Hannah could gather her thoughts and plan her actions. There was still no news about Leo, but she did manage to speak to Diana who was evasive and rather sharp with her.

"I really don't have to discuss why I've left my agent with you, Hannah. It's a matter I prefer not to broadcast."

"Was it anything to do with Joan's death? Or Leo Hawkins?"

"No, it was not. The whole universe does not revolve around that family, Hannah. Joan, as you know, was a dear friend, but my departure from Caroline's agency is a professional matter."

And with that Hannah had to be satisfied.

She looked at Janet's notes on the list she'd given her. So, Caroline Maston had been there. Why? Hannah assumed she'd been taking a director to see Joan in action on stage. He presumably was the person with her: Jeremy Gainey. She'd never heard of him, but that didn't make him an accessory to murder.

According to Janet's comments, Roger Priest was in shock and needed some medical treatment. Although it must have been terrible to discover Joan's body like that, his reaction seemed excessive. Unless… She looked back at the info Rory had sent through from one of the subs. There was some hint of a scandal that had been hushed up a few years ago. Still that didn't make him a murderer. But it did perhaps make him vulnerable. According to Janet's notes, DS Farnham had interviewed him.

She was going around in circles. All of this was conjecture and circumstance. She was no further forward when she left to collect Elizabeth from Linda and Dave's.

NEVILLE AND HIS family must have been watching out for their arrival, as he rushed out of the 1930s semi-detached house to help her with the car seat and bags. His daughters were clearly excited at the prospect of meeting Elizabeth, but waited patiently in the doorway. As Hannah walked up the path, Yvonne appeared behind them. Her smile was wide and welcoming. Hannah realised how pretty she was with her dark curly hair, and vivid blue eyes. Her bone structure was to die for. As her daughters moved aside for them to enter, Hannah saw that Yvonne was heavily pregnant. Maybe that's what gave her that wonderful glow.

She hugged Hannah. "Come in. Welcome to the mad house."

Elizabeth wriggled free from Hannah's arms and was immediately taken in hand by Charlotte and Katie, who led her into a room that was full of toys, bean bags and a dolls tea set ready on a small table.

"Don't worry," Yvonne said, noticing Hannah's look of concern. "We've tidied away any small items and toys that are too old for Elizabeth."

Hannah relaxed. Then it hit her with a rock hard force. Elizabeth was Paul's child. What would Yvonne make of that? Could she see a resemblance?

"Come through," said Neville, as he put the car seat into another room and shut the door.

The adults went into a large airy space, which was both a kitchen and dining room. One corner was furnished with comfy seats and overflowing bookshelves. One wall was taken up with patio doors overlooking the garden which seemed well-tended and, like everything else about the house, inviting.

"What would you like to drink, Hannah?" Neville had opened the fridge to put in the bottle of wine she had brought with her. "G and T?"

"That would be lovely."

Neville produced three glasses, but the third he filled with just ice, lime and tonic water. Yvonne took this and when they all had their drinks, she raised her glass.

"Welcome Hannah. It's lovely to meet you properly at last. I was beginning to think Neville didn't want to share you." Hannah smiled and sipped her drink. It seemed an odd thing to say. Yvonne then checked what was in the oven.

"Now, before I forget, this is what you asked me to find out for you." Neville handed her an envelope. "All fairly standard. But the will was written only a few months before Priscilla Preston died. Her previous will had left everything to a distant cousin somewhere. No one challenged the new will."

As much as Hannah would have liked to look through the papers there and then, she put the envelope in her bag. "Thank you Neville. That's really helpful."

"SO HOW'S THE book going now that Joan is no longer with us?"

They were sitting in comfortable chairs in their sitting room where the children were watching a video. Elizabeth, sitting between the two older girls, was entranced by *The Lady and The Tramp*. Hannah wondered about getting a pet, maybe a cat. She was pulled out of her reverie by Yvonne's question. She stared at her, then remembered she worked for a publishing company. It was a small and, from what she could judge, cliquey world.

"It's odd, to be honest. Joan's death has obviously raised a lot of interest and now Hallstone Books is keen to get the book published before anyone brings out an unauthorised version."

Yvonne nodded. "And you never know who might have been planning a book to be published in the wake of her death, anyway."

That was something Hannah hadn't considered. She wondered if Yvonne knew of such a book.

Neville looked as though he might be nodding off. However, he was obviously listening to them. "Not much Lord Gyles can do about that. Your advantage is you have access to all her first draft, papers and, presumably, her friends."

"But that wouldn't stop anyone else digging for dirt, and I expect there are some people who Joan upset or ignored over the years only to eager to besmirch her name now." Yvonne had her feet up on a stool. Neville reached over and took her hand. There was a silent communication between them that excluded Hannah. She looked at her watch. It was nearly four; she should be thinking about booking a cab home.

"Have you heard of any other potential books?" Hannah felt sick at the thought. She needed to concentrate on getting the manuscript finished. Lord Gyles would not be happy if they were pipped to the post.

"One or two." Hannah's mood plummeted. "You know the type of thing, written by showbiz hacks who just patch together articles and interviews. How far have you got?"

"Well, Hallstone Books had already agreed the synopsis and chapter plans with Joan and she had written the first draft. We had met several times so I could ask questions and get Joan to expand on some areas. Sometimes it's difficult not to get bogged down on the trivia. But we were nearly there before... before she died."

"Sounds as though you're almost ready to submit it." Yvonne smiled at her. "And remember, there will be an editor working with you. It's not your sole responsibility."

"Yes." Hannah was beginning to feel slightly better about the book. "I suppose the real problem is how we deal with her death. It's almost like the book is on hold until we find out whether she was killed and if so, by whom?"

Neville looked amused. "Always the journalist, Hannah."

Hannah managed a laugh. "It's ironic I was given this commission to keep me out of harm's way, but it seems to have stirred up yet another hornets' nest."

"If I were you," Yvonne said, "I'd hand in the manuscript and worry about the final chapter when it's needed. That way you'll be ready to go to press far sooner."

ON THE WAY home in the cab, Hannah went over the day in her mind. At first, she could only see Yvonne as the woman Paul had loved and lost. But as they chatted over lunch, compared notes on child-rearing and picky eaters, Hannah realised that whoever Paul had been in love with, it wasn't this version of Yvonne. He had been deluded. Hannah really liked Neville's wife and he had been the perfect host. Only as they were leaving and he was helping them into the car, did he comment on the current situation.

"Be careful, Hannah, won't you? And if you need any more help just ask. That's what I'm here for as your solicitor and, I hope, as a friend. And you know I'll always have your and Elizabeth's best interests at heart." He kissed her on the cheek and closed the car door.

As they drove off Neville waved from the roadside and Yvonne and her two daughters were framed in the doorway. For a moment she wanted to cry she felt so alone. But tomorrow was another day and right now she had to make sure Elizabeth didn't nod off in the car or she'd never get her to sleep at bedtime. The wheels on the bus went round and round... Just like her life. Her maudlin thoughts really were an indulgence. She had so much to be grateful for and it was about time she acknowledged the fact.

Safely home, Elizabeth had been happy to have her tea and bath before bed. "Which story would you like?" Hannah asked.

Her daughter went over to the bookshelves in her room and picked a book. It wasn't one they'd read recently, but at least it wasn't *Where's Spot?* Hannah smiled at how Elizabeth often wanted the same story over and over again. *Five Minutes Peace* would fit the bill perfectly. Soon, Elizabeth could keep her eyes open no longer and drifted into her private world. Hannah dimmed the light and went to her study.

Yvonne was right. The manuscript was almost there and Hannah needed to go through it for continuity and making sure the quotes she'd got went into the correct chapters. The publishing house had an editor lined up for Hannah to work with. She wasn't alone in this. There was a team. A small one, but dedicated. The final chapter could be added when she had worked it out. It would be good to move on. She'd been side-tracked too many times. Once the manuscript was sent in, she could concentrate on trying to find out what had really happened to Joan and why whoever murdered her had felt the need to try to kill her son as well. Strange, she thought, neither Yvonne or Neville had mentioned Leo today.

By the time Hannah went to bed she felt far more positive. One thing at a time. Tomorrow she would sort out the world. As she drifted off to sleep, she inhaled the smell of freesia and felt Leo's arms around her. Her body remembered his embrace. Would she ever experience his kiss again?

THIRTY-THREE

WHILE SHE WAS going through the last of Joan's photo albums, marking any for inclusion in the book, Hannah wondered again about Caroline Maston. There had to be more to her story. Why change her name from Caro Reynolds? Perhaps because of the link to her previous career? Yet the fingerless gloves were a bit of a give-away to anyone who knew her history. Or maybe not. Hannah was convinced there was more to the story. However, Joan Ballantyne obviously hadn't held a grudge, seeing as she was happy for her to be her agent after Priscilla Preston died.

She went downstairs to make some coffee, which she took into the dining room. On the long table, the photos Edith had taken after the funeral were laid out in a timeline. Hannah rearranged them into groups. The cast and crew all looked suitably sad. Wondering perhaps if, as the cliché had it, the show must go on. Apparently Joan Ballantyne returning to the stage was what filled the theatre for this little known play. The audiences loved her and she thrived on the adulation. No reason, it would seem, to end her life. So who did she see between the matinée and the evening performances?

Hannah scrutinised each shot. There was Sam Smith. It had been such a surprise when he appeared in some of the photos. But she couldn't imagine he'd got a job at the theatre in order to kill off the play's star. No one in that group, it seemed, had any sort of motive for killing Joan. But maybe they had the means and certainly the opportunity. Perhaps one of them was acting on the command of someone else.

The photos of family was a much smaller pile. Joan's sister Eileen and her husband, an accountant who looked after Joan's finances apparently, stayed at one table and didn't really circulate. Leo's ex-wife and two daughters were with them most of the time. Hannah went back to the day in her mind. Searching for any clue. Any hint.

Leo had given her a list of attendees and their relationship to his mother. On a photocopy, she'd scribbled some notes.

Hannah went through each photo looking for Caroline Maston in her distinctive, black silk fingerless gloves. One photo caught her on her own, back to a window, presumably surveying the room. She looked heartbroken, lost. For a moment no one was fawning around her. Her grief looked real. Hannah thought about her dealings with the agent. Was she worried about her portrayal in the book?

She was getting bogged down again. Her coffee was cold, so she went to make some more. As the water boiled, she watched the steam and remembered the description of a puff of smoke that erupted when Roger had moved the armchair on stage unaware that Joan's dead body would be exposed. An effect that added to the drama of the moment, for sure. Caroline Maston had, according to Janet, been on stage when she and the other officer arrived. And Caroline, as she now knew, had been a pyro-technician. However, a puff of smoke would have been simple for almost anyone to achieve.

Hannah looked at the odd photos that didn't fit into any of her groupings. Leo had also given Edith a list of attendees and had, apparently, underlined people who she should make a point of photographing. Edith had done this, but as she had explained to Hannah, she'd also followed her instincts. Some of the compositions were really arty and she'd made best use of the décor of the Lillian Baylis bar as a backdrop. Hannah was admiring one, which showed a portrait of Laurence Olivier, when she realised that, to one side, Sam Smith was in a deep conversation with someone she wouldn't have thought he would have been that friendly with. It was time to give Sam a call.

HANNAH DRUMMED HER fingers on her desk. Sam Smith was not at work and no one at the theatre had his home number according to the stage door manager. That was bollocks. A word she rarely used, but in this instance fitted the bill precisely.

She rang Sir David's number and got through to a recorded message. She almost didn't leave her name and number but then did. She could always call back this afternoon if no one contacted her.

Ten minutes later her phone had rung. "Hannah, how can I help you?"

He gave her not just a number for Sam, but also his address. "He hasn't been in for a few days apparently. Phoned in sick, I think."

"Thank you, that's very helpful. Can I ask you—why do people not like him?"

"I have no idea. But why wouldn't they?"

"Oh, just something someone said. But Joan's death may have spooked them."

"Perhaps. How's the book going?"

"Nearly there. I just hope it does Joan justice."

"Justice. A strange word to use, but I'm sure you've done your best and Lord Gyles wouldn't have engaged you if he didn't think you were up to the job. He's not exactly known for his charitable acts. He's a businessman who will want his pound of flesh. I shall look forward to reading it."

HANNAH THOUGHT ABOUT Sir David's words as she sat in a cab on the way to Sam Smith's home. She had bought some flowers for him. Visiting the sick was her excuse. She wondered about the home he and Marti had set up. She was teaching in a private school now. Did her employers know about her past profession? None of their business, she supposed. Her thoughts went back to the first time she'd met Marti in a greasy spoon near King's Cross. She'd been reading George Eliot's *Felix Holt*, which had surprised Hannah, and Marti certainly had not been happy or willing to talk to her. But she had come up trumps on the information she'd subsequently given her. Hannah sighed—that all seemed such a long time ago. Was it really only last year? When she had met Tom—and Caroline.

The car pulling up outside a terraced house brought her back to the present. She surveyed the road. It was a quiet street off the main thoroughfares. Not a place she'd find a taxi easily. "Could you wait for me here? It's on account."

"Suits me, luv." He switched off the engine, picked up the newspaper from the passenger seat and began the crossword. As she got out of the car, Hannah wondered how Sam and Marti had managed to get a house like this—a little two up two down in a pretty mews. Hannah had no time to consider more, as the door opened before she'd had a chance to ring the bell.

"Hannah, what on earth are you doing here?"

Marti was dressed in a smart grey suit and a yellow roll neck jumper. She was on her way out but looked at her watch. "Come in." She stood aside. The front door opened on to the sitting room, which was small, but furnished to make the most of the space available. Fitted cupboards in the alcoves with bookshelves above. Paperbacks mainly.

"Sit down would you like something to drink. Tea, coffee?"

"No, I don't want to hold you up." She handed Marti the flowers. "I heard Sam wasn't feeling well…"

Hannah couldn't read the expression that clouded Marti's face. "I wouldn't know—I haven't seen him for a few days."

"He hasn't been into work," she said gently.

"Oh God. I told him not to get mixed up in that crowd."

"What crowd? He doesn't seem too popular at the Vic."

"He wouldn't be."

"What makes you say that?"

"The job at the theatre was just a cover. He was ferreting out information for someone."

"What sort of information?" Hannah was intrigued.

"I've no idea. It was one of his drinking mates who put him up for it. All cloak and dagger, and you know how Sam likes that."

Hannah nodded. "So how long exactly has he been missing for?"

Marti gave her a sharp look. "I didn't say he was missing. I said I hadn't seen him."

"So you know where he is?"

"I've a fair idea."

"Can you tell me?"

Marti stared out of the window. When she turned her face to Hannah, she looked terrified. "Hannah, you really don't want to get mixed up in any of this."

"Any of what?"

"Sam's a wheeler and dealer. You know how he likes to squirrel away information. Think about how you met him."

A ghost of a smile crossed Hannah's face. Sam had worked at Lost Property at King's Cross Station. He'd been Tom's informant. And he'd helped her.

"I bumped into him at London Bridge a while ago. In May. He seemed happy then with his new job and his new living arrangements." She smiled at Marti. "He was so proud you'd got your degree." It was then Hannah noticed a photo of Marti in cap and gown, taken at her graduation. For a moment a vision of Marti in a very different outfit came to mind and Hannah blinked it away.

"Yes, well, none of that stopped him. I don't know why he took that job at the Vic, but I've a fair idea it wasn't for the wages there."

"So how long haven't you seen him for?"

"Three days."

"Isn't that unusual? Did he call you?"

"Yes once. He said he had a bit of business to see to and he wouldn't be home, but I wasn't to worry."

"And are you? Are you worried?"

"What do you think? I'm scared out of my mind."

"So what can I do? Have you contacted the police?"

Marti shook her head.

As if on cue, Hannah's mobile rang. "Excuse me for a moment." She took the call. DI Benton sounded grim.

"I need to discuss something that's come up, Hannah. Are you at home?"

"No, but I will be in about half an hour."

"Okay. I'll see you then."

"Sorry about that, Marti. Look, here's my card with my number. Call me any time. And if I hear anything I'll let you know."

Marti opened the front door for her. "Just be careful, Hannah."

"I will. Believe me, I don't need any more complications in my life." A current of understanding passed between them and Hannah got into her waiting cab. Marti didn't see her wave goodbye as she had already turned to lock the door.

So what the hell had Sam got mixed up in? It must be bad for Marti to be so worried.

Thirty-four

DI MIKE BENTON was sitting in an unmarked car with a driver beside him. They both got out as Hannah arrived. The DI smiled. He looked even smarter these days and his new glasses gave him more gravitas. "Hannah this is DS Tony Farnham." The man nodded at her. The name rang a bell. Of course! She remembered Janet telling her about the DS who had arrived at The Old Vic on the night Joan Ballantyne had died. The one who had made a point of interviewing Roger Priest.

"Come in."

She unlocked the door and switched off the alarm. She could see the sergeant taking in her security arrangements as they followed her into the sitting room.

"Would you like some tea or coffee?"

The DS looked as though he was going to accept, but Mike answered for them both. "No thanks." They sat next to each other on one sofa while she perched on the other. The sergeant fished out a pack of cigarettes from his pocket.

"I'd rather you didn't smoke in my home, Sergeant."

He looked furiously at Mike, who in turn looked at the photos of Elizabeth. "What great photos Hannah—she looks so much like you."

Hannah smiled. "Edith Holland took them as a surprise when I was in hospital."

There was a moment of silence as they both remembered why she had been hospitalised.

DS Farnham had put away his cigarettes. "Well, it's Miss Holland, we've come to see you about actually."

"Oh?" The DS had his notebook open and was taking notes. She noticed how stubby his nicotine-stained fingers were and his nails were bitten to the quick.

"Have you seen her recently?"

"No, not since we went to Joan Ballantyne's flat together and met Leo Hawkins there. She'd left by the time you arrived."

"Spoken to her?"

"Only to thank her for the photos of Joan's flat that she sent me. Look what is this about?"

"She appears to have gone missing."

"Missing? What do you mean?"

The DS looked up. "I'd have thought that was obvious. Missing, as in no one has seen her for several days."

Hannah glared at him. "I'm perfectly aware of what the word means sergeant, I was asking about the context." Her icy tone would have been enough to quell a riot, but the sergeant seemed oblivious.

Mike Benton looked amused and clearly had no intention of rescuing this cocky sergeant he'd been saddled with. Tony opened his mouth, but must have thought better of continuing the line of conversation, so said nothing.

"Her sister reported her missing. She hasn't been at her flat…"

Her sister? "What about her studios?"

"Not there either."

"Maybe she's gone off on an assignment. Or away seeing friends? I really don't know her well enough to say."

"Have you been to her studios?"

"Yes once. After Joan Ballantyne's funeral."

Mike nodded. "We don't think she's been there recently."

"Mail piled by the door…"

"Yes, thank you sergeant." Mike looked as though he'd like to throttle Farnham. "But it does look as though someone else has been there."

"How do you mean?" The sergeant looked about to say something else, but Mike spoke first.

"Looks as though someone was looking for something specific."

Hannah looked at them blankly. "I'm not sure what this has to do with me, Inspector." Hannah felt a touch of formality was needed.

Mike looked uncomfortable. "The only files that seem to have been disturbed were all connected to Joan Ballantyne. It looks as though they were looking for something in particular. Of course, we don't know if they found what they were looking for."

Hannah could feel the muscles in her stomach tighten. She felt sick. Was Edith's disappearance her fault? What danger had she led to her door? Her scar was itching again, and she longed to scratch and scratch…

"Hannah?" Mike's voice came from the end of a long tunnel. "Hannah are you ok? Go and get her a glass of water, Tony." Farnham looked about to protest. "Kitchen. At the end of the hall. Now."

Hannah felt herself falling, but Mike had moved quickly and pushed her gently onto the sofa, where she had been perched on the arm. "Take deep breaths."

The sergeant returned from his mission. "Here, sip this. Slowly." Mike's arm supported her and gradually the room stopped spinning.

"Sorry I don't know…"

"You've had a shock, miss." Hannah thought she'd like to shock him with a powerful bolt of electricity.

"When did you last eat?" Benton didn't wait for an answer. "Sergeant, there's a café across the road. Go and buy some sandwiches for us all. Might as well eat while we can." He saw the officer hesitate, pulled out his wallet and took out a twenty-pound note. "Get a receipt."

"Right guv."

When the front door closed behind his sergeant, Mike let out a huge sigh. "God, give me strength."

She was feeling better and grateful to Mike. "Shall we go into the kitchen and make some coffee?"

He followed her through to the rear of the house. "Do you miss having Janet around?"

"I do, although we do see each other quite regularly."

"She's a good officer."

"And she was a good nanny." Hannah smiled ruefully. "I miss listening to her playing with Elizabeth. She's at nursery now. Life's full of changes."

"Yeah, I remember when our two started nursery. Suddenly they have part of their existence which doesn't include you."

"That's exactly it. Sometimes, when we're out, someone will say hello to her and I haven't a clue who they are." The kettle boiled and Hannah turned away to make the coffee, glad of a moment to get to grips with her emotions.

The doorbell rang. "That will be lunch." Mike went out and returned with the officer. "Okay to eat in here, Hannah?"

"Of course. There's a loo through there if you want to wash your hands."

When Mike was out of the room, Tony smirked. "You seem to have the DI wound round your little finger."

"I beg your pardon." Frosty was Hannah's default position with this horrible man.

"I just mean…" He stopped as Mike returned.

"Yes, what did you mean?" Mike could do frosty too.

"Nothing sir."

"Good, or you'll be eating on your own in the car."

Hannah almost laughed. Mike sounded like he was telling off a stroppy teenager. She put plates, mugs and the coffee, milk and sugar on the table then helped herself to a sandwich.

"Thanks. I needed this."

Mike looked at her waiting for her to continue. Farnham was too busy stuffing his face to notice his expression.

"Edith is the second person I've heard about today who seems to have gone missing."

"Should we know about the first one?"

Hannah could have kicked herself. "Maybe later. But I may be able to help you with the situation at Edith's studios."

Tony had finished his sandwich. Sating his appetite hadn't improved his manner. "I just love amateur sleuths. What do you suggest Miss Marple?"

Mike looked as though he was going to burst a blood vessel. "DS Farnham, we'll be leaving soon, please wait for me in the car."

Farnham's face was a confused picture of insolence and rebellion. Common sense and self-preservation won out, and he left.

"Sorry about that Hannah. He's enough to try the patience of a saint." He grinned. "And we both know I'm no saint."

"You and I both." She topped up their coffee. "Thanks for lunch."

"We all have to eat. Saints and sinners alike. Now what were you saying about helping with Edith Holland's studio before we were so rudely interrupted?"

"I have copies of all the photos Edith has taken connected to Joan Ballantyne. We could go through the ones at the studios and see what's missing?" Mike was silent. "If that would be of help?"

Mike breathed deeply. "I was hoping you were going to say something like that. Thanks Hannah. Could you come with us now? I promise to muzzle the idiot."

MIKE OPENED THE rear door for Hannah and sat in the front passenger seat. "Drive by the nick on our way to Edith Holland's studios, please Sergeant."

"Yes guv."

No one spoke on the way, until Mike said, "Pull up at the front entrance."

When the car came to a standstill, Mike got out of the car and went round to open the driver's door. "You can go to the incident room and follow up any leads and check that all the info has been input into the system." He didn't say leads to what but Hannah could see the DS was furious.

"But I thought..."

"I'll be back later. Make sure everything is up to date."

Tony Farnham looked as though he'd like to argue his case, but one look at his inspector's face told him it would be wasted energy. He just about remembered enough of his manners to turn to Hannah. "Nice to meet you." She had the feeling that was not at all what he meant.

Mike got in the driver's seat. "Want to sit up front so we can talk?"

Hannah changed places and Mike gunned the engine and sped forward. "Sorry about that twat."

"May I be indiscreet?"

Mike laughed. "Go on."

"Janet told me something about the DS who attended The Old Vic the night Joan Ballantyne died."

"Ye-es."

"She mentioned something to him and he was totally dismissive."

Mike shook his head. "He needs to get a grip of himself." He didn't ask what Janet had mentioned and Hannah didn't say. She had an idea that he already knew.

WHEN THEY ARRIVED at the arches, Mike parked and retrieved some keys from his pocket. "You've got keys to the studios?"

"How else did you think we were going to get in?"

How indeed?

"Actually, when we came here to check that Edith wasn't here, the door had been forced. We had a locksmith change the locks.

There's a lot of expensive equipment here…" He put on some gloves and handed a pair to Hannah.

Inside felt damp and airless. Mike switched on the lights and they walked over to the large table where photos were splayed out with no concern for order or context. Hannah felt the nausea rise again. Edith was so careful with her work, it was painful to see some of it like this. "She will have the negatives stowed away somewhere. All these seem to be copies of prints."

"Shall we get them into some sort of order before trying to work out what's missing—if anything."

She and Mike worked in companionable silence until he said, "That's a good one of you."

Hannah looked up. It wasn't. "Sequence, Mike."

Eventually, they had piles of photos in numerical order. "Numbers 15, 23 and 56 are missing."

Hannah produced her set of prints. They both stared at the first, willing inspiration to enlighten them. It was a group of people taken quite early in the proceedings. Mainly theatre staff that hadn't gone to the funeral service, but had organised the Lillian Baylis bar for the wake. And there, chatting away to someone she didn't know or recognise was a man who had been very much on her mind.

She pointed a finger at him. "That's Sam Smith. He used to work in Lost Property at King's Cross Station. He was one of Tom Jordan's snouts." She'd managed to say Tom's name without faltering. "Then I bumped into him at London Bridge Station in May. I didn't see him at the wake. Just after I had spoken to the ASM, Sam rang asking me not to say I knew him and that he'd avoided me at the wake. Too late, as I'd already asked the ASM about him, and he'd described him as a creep. I didn't say I knew him well. According to his partner, Marti, he's been missing for three days."

"When did you speak to her?"

"This morning. She said he'd got mixed up with some people who were trouble."

Mike stared at her. "Shit. A mudlarker found a body this morning. Farnham and I picked up the call. No ID on the corpse, but if I'm not very much mistaken, he's our man. He hadn't been in the river long by his appearance."

Hannah's tears ran unchecked. Whatever Sam had got mixed up in now he had helped her when she…

"I'm sorry," she sniffed. "I didn't even know him very well, but he was kind to me in an 'any friend of Tom's is a friend of mine' type of way." Mike had handed her a handkerchief. She wiped her eyes and blew her nose. "Shall we look at the other two photos?"

Mike looked concerned. "You okay with that?"

Hannah attempted a smile and placed numbers 23 and 56 alongside 15. Photo 23 revealed Hannah sitting with Diana Stowbridge and in the last one she was with Leo Hawkins. The DI's attention went back to number 15. "You're in this one too."

Hannah looked again. In the first one she appeared to be staring across the room at Sam but actually, she remembered, it was Caroline Maston who was in the group he was chatting with that had caught her attention. Hannah closed her eyes and her mind went back to the wake. Edith and she had travelled in the taxi with Caroline. They had walked in together, but Caroline had immediately started working the room with scarcely a backward glance at Hannah and Edith.

"Hannah?"

She shivered. "I think someone just walked over my grave. Just a saying," she added seeing Benton's concerned look. "That woman there is Caroline Maston, Joan Ballantyne's agent. I'm surprised she would bother chatting to the stagehands, but maybe I've misjudged her. Leo had just introduced me to Sir David Powys, the director at the Vic…"

"And you can't think why whoever stole the photos would take those particular ones?"

"What apart from the obvious that one person was attacked and left for dead and another has just turned up drowned in the Thames?"

THIRTY-FIVE

HANNAH HAD NO sooner arrived home, than her phone rang. It was Rory. "I don't know whether you've heard about the body being washed up by Tower Bridge this morning?"

Hannah could feel the shock waves through her body. "I do know as it happens, but why on earth would *The News* be interested?"

"We weren't at first, then we had a tip-off that the dead person may have had a connection to Joan Ballantyne."

"What?" Hannah couldn't believe what she was hearing. She knew from previous research that bodies got washed ashore, once a week or so, somewhere along the two hundred odd miles stretch of the Thames. However, it was rare for those discoveries to make the news even locally; most simply became forgotten victims of the river. They were certainly not usually national news stories. And not this quickly. Sam hadn't even been formally identified as far as she knew. When she and Mike left the studios, he had been going to pick up a female officer before going to see Marti. It didn't make sense.

"You're not going to like this, but the person who gave us the information mentioned your name."

Hannah could feel the remembered terror coursing through her body. Her scar ached. She felt dizzy. With a supreme effort she took a deep calming breath.

"Hannah? Are you still there?"

"Yes, sorry Rory. Could you hold fire on this? I need to check something and I may need to come into the office?"

"Okay. Anything I can do in the meantime?"

SHE RANG MIKE Benton's mobile number little expecting him to answer the call, but at least she could leave a message that only he would hear. She certainly wasn't going to contact the incident room. She wanted nothing further to do with DS Farnham. To her surprise, Mike answered after the second ring. "DI Benton."

"Mike, it's Hannah. I need to speak to you urgently and in complete privacy."

There was a pause. "Okay. I'm about fifteen minutes away. Shall I call in?"

"Thanks."

Hannah hadn't time to collect her thoughts before the phone rang again.

"Hi Hannah, I think you may need a babysitter for later. I'll be over a.s.a.p." The line went dead before she could respond.

DI BENTON ARRIVED first. Whoever his driver was remained in the car. "So tell me." His expression was grim and Hannah wondered if he was annoyed with her. Then she remembered where he'd been.

"How was Marti?"

"In pieces. Poor woman."

"Come into the garden, there's something I want to show you." She placed two fingers to her lips and he followed her through the kitchen into the garden.

"I had a call from Rory at *The News*. They'd had a tip-off about the body found at Tower Bridge. The person who rang in mentioned my name. Someone was trying to discredit me, Mike. I have told no one about anything I've done or people I've seen today. The leak must have come from a member of your team."

Benton said nothing but looked furious. It was cold and the sun was going down. Hannah shivered. It was horrible to think anyone was out to get her. The intimidation was escalating. She'd upset someone with the means to get to her.

"Why are we outside Hannah?"

"I haven't had the house checked for bugs recently."

"Right."

"I may be being paranoid but your sergeant's antipathy towards me today made me wonder…"

For a moment Mike's expression reminded her of when they first met. He had interviewed her just after she'd discovered her friend Liz Rayman's dead body in the crypt at St John's in Waterloo. He had been hateful then. Had she triggered a similar response?

"I'll hang him out to dry. The little shit." Mike spat out the words. "Sorry Hannah. If he has anything to do with this…" He looked up at the sky. "I wonder why he was so antagonistic towards you. Somehow it seemed personal."

"Very."

"Right. Oh, by the way, I contacted Janet in case you were wondering. She's here officially but keep that to yourself. I assumed you'd want to go into *The News*?" She nodded. Why was Janet going to be here officially? What was Mike not telling her? "Right. I'm going to brief our press office to send out a release about the body. There'll be no mention of a name or any connections. Just a catchall asking if anyone saw anything type of thing. Also I'll send someone round to sweep your house for bugs…"

"That's not necessary. I usually ask…"

"Maybe a change is needed." He didn't elaborate. "Let's go inside, it's getting chilly out here." His smile was reassuring. "Well done, and don't worry I'll sort that leak and if it is who we think it is…" He left Hannah to imagine his fate.

IT WAS ONLY when she was in a car going to *The News* offices that she suddenly thought of Edith's cameras. She hadn't seen them. Were they missing from the studios? Maybe they were at her flat. She made a mental note to ask DI Benton.

Janet had arrived soon after Mike departed. She wasn't in uniform. "I was told to come in civvies to avoid drawing attention to your house. I'll collect and look after Elizabeth."

Her attitude was almost imperceptibly different, but Hannah sensed the change in her. Her professionalism. On duty, she wasn't Janet who used to be her nanny. And that was how it should be, Hannah thought.

DI MIKE BENTON stormed into the incident room and marched straight up to DS Farnham's desk. "Any updates of note?"

The officer in charge of the system answered for them all. "Nothing major, guv, and everything has been entered on HOLMES."

"Thank you." His sergeant seemed to be inspecting his nails. No one else spoke. "Right I suggest you all finish for today and we'll start early tomorrow morning. I've had the press office issue a release on the body washed up by Tower Bridge. Maybe someone saw something."

Farnham coughed. "I thought you'd decided to keep it under wraps for the time being, Guv."

"I had, but something else has come up. Come into my office for a moment." Mike forced himself to smile and Farnham followed him into his corner office and made to sit down.

"Keep standing, Sergeant." Farnham looked confused. "What was all that this morning with Hannah Weybridge?"

"All what, guv?"

"Don't play the smart arse with me. You were intentionally rude, unpleasant and…"

"Give over, Guv. She's just a tabloid hack."

Benton had to breathe deeply to maintain his composure. "A 'tabloid hack', as you put it, who has helped solve several major cases and expose some pretty nasty criminals."

"If you say so, sir." Farnham's confidence had diminished but only a little. The "Sir" sounded sarcastic. Did he think he was beyond reproach?

Benton shook his head. "What is your problem, Tony?"

His sergeant remained silent, hands in pockets looking as though he didn't have a care in the world. Mike sighed. "Why did you leave the office to make a call from a phone box?"

"I didn't."

"You're not making this any better for yourself, Tony. You were seen."

Farnham fidgeted uncomfortably. "It was personal."

"Really? It wasn't a call to a newspaper about the river body?"

Farnham's face changed colour from pale to red. "No, Guv. Like I said, it was personal."

Benton ignored the comment. "And what made you link it to Hannah Weybridge? We had no idea who it was. Or did you know? And if you did—and I suggest you think very carefully before answering—would you mind telling me why you didn't inform me as your senior officer?"

Farnham stared at the floor.

"Hand over your pocketbook."

Farnham looked up. "What?"

"What 'sir'. Hand over your pocketbook and your warrant card. You are suspended pending investigation."

"You can't do this." But his tone was sullen, defeated.

"I've already cleared it with the DCI."

Farnham looked as though he might cry. Benton wasn't moved. "You will be contacted by CIB about what happens next, and you'll need to speak to your federation rep. Now, listen carefully and do exactly as I say. I will walk you to your desk. I want you to collect anything personal and then you will leave the building. Don't make a fuss. Is that understood?"

Farnham did as he was told. All his previous cockiness had deserted him. If Benton hadn't known better, he'd have felt sorry for him. He watched him leave; an officer who had been previously briefed to follow the sergeant left soon after. Benton walked back into his office and sat with his head in his hands. Before taking up his new post, he had been warned there was a problem person in the team. Two possible suspects had been named but not confirmed. They hadn't been questioned. Today's events confirmed his suspicions. His first major case as a DI and this had to happen. He prayed he hadn't made the wrong decision.

THIRTY-SIX

RORY WAS WAITING for her in reception when she arrived. He grinned. "I was told we could use the board room. We'll go through what we know and then call George if necessary." They stepped into the lift, but said nothing.

He had arranged for coffee and sandwiches, plus there was a bowl of fruit. They sat at the corner of the large table.

"So what's happening?"

"What isn't?" She felt defeated and tired.

"Let's start with today."

Hannah stared at the picture on the wall opposite. "This morning, I went to see Sam Smith…" She told him about seeing Marti, who had told her Sam had not been home in three days.

"So why did you think Sam was important?"

"I didn't really. I wanted to find out why he was working at the theatre. It just seemed a strange coincidence. The ASM, Charlie, told me he thought Sam was creepy, which I thought was odd, as he'd always been kind to me. He also thought he was snooping around for stories to sell to the press. I don't think that was the case." She paused, frowning. "There seem to be connections that I can't see. A pattern… Then DI Benton rang and arranged to meet me at my house. His sergeant behaved in a hostile and frankly rude manner towards me. They'd come to tell me that Edith Holland had been reported missing by her sister."

"The photographer?"

Hannah nodded. Helping herself to a sandwich, she filled Rory in on the details. Rory made notes.

"The tip-off about the body found by Tower Bridge was from one of my regular police informants, but he made a point of saying to ask Hannah Weybridge about him."

"I didn't even know about a body then. It was only when we were going through the photos in Edith's studio, that Mike made the connection. The body hadn't had any identification on it, but hadn't been in the water long apparently. It was strange that DI Benton and

Farnham had actually been at the scene shortly after the body was found. I never found out why."

She stared at the bowl of fruit as though it would reveal everything she needed to know.

"It's all such a mess. All these things that have been happening to try and intimidate me." Rory made no comment. Her voice betrayed her anger. "Two people have died connected to The Old Vic, Leo Hawkins has been beaten and left for dead, and now Edith is missing."

"Why do you think she's missing?"

"Her sister reported her as missing. She'd not been at her flat or her studios. But I really don't know her well enough to …"

"Exactly. She could just be away on a commission. Or a few days holiday. Have you met the sister?"

"No. I didn't even know she had one. She never talked about family, or friends for that matter. She seemed quite insular really."

"Maybe she has a man friend tucked away."

"I hope she has."

Rory changed tack. "How's the book coming along?"

"Okay. I've printed it out and am now reading through it again."

"Any great revelations?"

Hannah laughed. "Joan dishes the dirt a few times. It will be up to the editor and legal team to check those. There are some dodgy characters and connections but nothing to get yourself killed for, I wouldn't think. Or to kill yourself for."

"So you definitely think it wasn't suicide then?"

Hannah sighed. "No. Not unless it was by accident."

Rory looked down at his notes. "Maybe it was."

"Was what?"

"An accident, which set in motion a series of events…"

"That's a bit of a stretch, isn't it?" Hannah was unconvinced. "Perhaps she was killed to get at a third party. Like the backers, but they're difficult to pin down."

"You're right. So what do you want to do? You have the lead on the body."

"Not sure I can use that information."

Her phone rang and she listened to DI Benton's voice telling her Farnham had been suspended. "Don't go public with it, Hannah. Don't identify Sam Smith. Not yet. Please."

She agreed and the call ended. She selected an orange and smiled at Rory. "And by the way just so you don't have to pull the 'a journalist never reveals his sources' trick, Benton confirmed the leak was Farnham. He's been suspended."

Rory expressed no surprise. "So what do we do?"

"I'd rather find out what links Sam to all this—if anything—before naming him. Whoever killed him probably didn't expect his body to be discovered so soon, and they obviously went to the trouble of removing anything that would identify him. Let's keep them guessing."

"Ok, we'll go along with the release from the police. Small news item, etcetera."

Hannah finished the orange and wiped her hands on a serviette. "Of course, the interesting thing is that Tony Farnham must have known who he was to link him to me, however tenuously. And he kept that from his senior officer."

There was a knock on the door. John, one of the subs, came in. "Sorry Rory but you said you wanted this as soon as... oh hi, Hannah. How are you?"

"I'm fine, thanks." She smiled as he left the room.

"So what couldn't wait?"

Rory flipped through the pages. "I had John dig up anything he could on Farnham. I try to have some background on any officer who feeds us stories. Just in case. It looks as though Mr Farnham likes to gamble."

"So?"

"So that makes him vulnerable. Especially as he's in debt to— Jesus why are people so bloody stupid. He's put his whole career on the line for... Wait a minute. I know him from somewhere else. Not betting." He tapped his head with his pen. "If I'm right—way back, his family had links to some of the biggest gangsters in London at one time. The Downs Mob. They went legit or found a way of seeming so. Laundering their money..."

"Through theatres..." And James Fentonbury had pointed the finger at them.

JANET WAS READING in the sitting room when Hannah arrived home. There was a welcoming aroma of food.

"Everything okay?" Hannah was so glad to be home with Janet here.

"Elizabeth is fine, bathed and tucked up in bed."

"Have you eaten?"

"No, I was waiting for you. I took the liberty of raiding your fridge, but I brought the wine with me." She smiled as she handed a glass to her former employer. They had been through so much together. An only child, Hannah was beginning to think this is what it might feel like to have a sister.

Hannah took a gulp. "You're a life saver, Janet. I'll just look in on Elizabeth."

When she returned to the kitchen, Janet had laid the table ready and taken the pasta bake out of the oven and the salad from the fridge. There was crusty bread and cheese to follow.

"Wow! What a feast."

Janet beamed. "More fun cooking for two."

Hannah raised her glass. "I'll drink to that. Thank you. Are you on or off duty now?"

"Not sure you're ever off duty on the job." Hannah took this as a subtle hint and helped herself to the food.

"This is delicious. I've only had sandwiches all day. The ones from the café across the road were quite nice actually, but delivered with such bad grace."

Janet finished her mouthful. "I heard that a certain DS didn't cover himself with glory."

"That's an understatement. It's funny, because when I first met Mike Benton he was grumpy and unpleasant and I know why now. He had been separated from his wife. He was miserable and it was nothing to do with me. But with this guy, it was different. Like it was personal."

"Perhaps it was. And probably had nothing to do with Joan Ballantyne. He's a bigot, that's for sure." They had made short work of the pasta and salad.

"I'm not sure I can manage cheese as well." Hannah sat back. "Shall we finish the wine in the sitting room? Leave all this," she said, as Janet made to start clearing away.

"How's your mother?" Hannah asked as they occupied a sofa each. Hannah had her feet up.

"Remarkably well. Living with my aunt obviously suits her, and when I visit, she actually tries really hard to be… I'm not sure really.

She knows how much she upset me but she's over the moon that I'm back in the police."

Hannah smiled, remembering the photos of Janet in uniform that her mother had taken down from the wall when she visited. "And your sister?"

"She's getting married, would you believe. In December. A Christmas wedding."

"How does that make you feel?"

"Off the hook." She laughed. Hannah missed that chuckle. "With a bit of luck, she'll get pregnant soon after and my mother's world will be complete."

They'd finished the wine and Hannah was tempted to open another bottle.

"Right, I'm going to love you and leave you. Early start tomorrow and I expect you're exhausted. What time do you take Elizabeth to nursery?"

Hannah yawned. The food and wine had relaxed her and she hoped an early night would restore her spirits. "About nine usually, unless I have to be somewhere early. I like to have some morning time with her. I miss hearing you two playing and chatting during the day."

Janet's expression looked raw. "So do I."

"But that couldn't go on for ever, and I am delighted you're back doing the job you love."

Hannah saw her to the door and quickly locked up behind her so she didn't see Janet pause by a car parked on the opposite side of the road.

THIRTY-SEVEN

"I WON'T DO IT." Fran looked at her husband defiantly. "Whatever mess you've got yourself into is of your own making. Not mine."

The punch caught her off guard and she reeled backwards. Fortunately, the sofa broke her fall. He'd hit her before. Not for a while now, it was true. But when he got himself into trouble, he always took it out on her. He never hit her where a bruise would show and she was too ashamed to tell anyone. One time she'd fallen badly and had broken her wrist. He had been so contrite. At the hospital, he was the epitome of a loving husband. "She must have tripped on a toy…"

"You didn't see what happened?"

"No I was…"

"On the phone. He was on the phone and had his back to me." The lie had tripped off her tongue. Another nail in the coffin of their marriage.

The nurse had accompanied her to the X-ray department and she'd winced as she sat down. "Where else are you hurt?" The nurse had looked at her with what Fran had assumed to be pity. "Is there anything else you want to tell me? Would you like me to call the police? It can be done discreetly."

She had been appalled. "No please don't. I'm fine, honestly."

Her mind came back to the present. How had she got into this situation? He was towering over her. "And don't think you can go running back to your fancy family."

She almost laughed in his face, but that would provoke him even more. Going to her family was furthest from her mind. The shame of admitting she'd made a mistake—that her husband was a bully who sometimes became violent—was something she couldn't face.

He yanked her up by her wrist, pulling her close to him so she could feel his breath on her neck. "You will do this. You owe me that much."

"I don't owe you anything."

He moved so quickly. He yanked her head back by her hair. "You're hurting me."

"Obviously, not enough…"

THIRTY-EIGHT

BY THE TIME Hannah got into bed, her anxieties were back. What on earth had Sam got himself mixed up with? Poor Marti must be beside herself. Should she phone her? Maybe Marti would contact her. She wouldn't have known about her meeting with Benton. She willed herself to relax and not think about Edith. Dear God, please don't let her become another victim. Janet hadn't mentioned her. Perhaps that was a good sign.

She turned her pillow over for the cooler side. She still felt anxious. Apprehensive. Unknown people were working against her. And a police officer had been involved. A corrupt officer. One who had links to the Downs Mob, who may or may not have had money invested in *Lady Heston Regrets*. Which brought her back to Joan Ballantyne's death. And the brutal assault on Leo.

Her mind was in overdrive. She was being sucked in deeper and deeper. What was it the therapist she had consulted some time ago had suggested? Yes, the arithmetic exercise. Think of a large number—say 27794—and keep subtracting an odd number like seventeen. The numbers always differed, but the effect was the same; it was impossible to think about anything else while concentrating on the numbers. Eventually she drifted into sleep.

HANNAH WOKE WITH a start. For a moment, she didn't know where she was. Her dream had been so vivid. She was...

"Mama! Mama!" The imperious call of her daughter brought her to the present.

"Coming darling." She looked at the bedside clock. 7.30. She couldn't believe she'd slept so long and so deeply. Pulling on her dressing gown, she went into Elizabeth's bedroom.

Elizabeth was standing up in her cot-bed, pointing at the window. "Look!" She smiled. "Look Mama." Hannah could see nothing, but an overwhelming scent of freesia filled the room.

She could hardly cross-examine a toddler, so she just picked her up and gave her a cuddle. "Tell me what you can see."

Elizabeth frowned. "Gone. Gone now." And with that Hannah had to be satisfied.

IT WAS WELL after nine when mother and daughter were ready to leave the house and make their way to the nursery. Janet followed at a distance, confident Hannah wouldn't spot her. It was amazing what people didn't notice when they weren't expecting to see someone.

Fran had also been waiting. She'd wanted to time her arrival to coincide with Hannah's so she'd been waiting by the corner shop, which was also a sub-post office. This gave her some cover, as it was pension day and there were lots of people eager to cash their Giros.

Harry was getting grumpy waiting in his buggy and there were only so many verses of *The Farmer's in his Den* she could use to distract him. Eventually she made out Hannah walking towards the nursery from the opposite direction and set off. "Here we go Harry."

Her son turned towards her beaming. "Lizbet." His tone was joyful as he pointed to his little friend.

JANET TOOK THE camera out of her rucksack and, partially concealed by a van, managed to get some shots as the two women greeted each other at the nursery gate. She couldn't hear their conversation but took individual close-ups of their faces. Hannah didn't seem as pleased to see the other woman, who was... Janet recognised Fran. They'd been at the same primary school. Even in the same class, although they were never friends. Not many kids wanted to be friends with someone whose dad was a police officer. And certainly not Fran Croxton.

Janet made some notes while the two women were inside the nursery and radioed through to the station. When Fran reappeared, she tailed her to a shop on a road off Lordship Lane. She was surprised to see Fran produce some keys and open up, then smiled when she saw the signage: Croxton Cakes and Catering.

HANNAH FELT FRAN had steamrollered her. She didn't want to meet her for a drink but couldn't think of a polite way to decline. The best she could do was delay it until the following week, pleading pressure of work. Fran had had to accept that, although she didn't look too happy and Hannah wondered why not. However, she didn't have time to waste.

HANNAH HAD CHECKED through the floppy disks Joan had originally given her. She had transferred the content on to her own computer and had worked on that, always backing up at the end of each working session. The original disks were in safekeeping at Hallstone Books. Something niggled at the back of her mind. The box of memorabilia that she had been through was under her desk. One last look, she thought, then, she could send that off as well.

She checked every item off on the original list she'd made. Everything was in order. Except for the floppy disk. She was sure Joan had only given her two. And she couldn't remember seeing an extra in this box. Maybe her mind was playing tricks on her, especially after everything that had happened yesterday and then having Fran on her case. There was only one thing to do. She slotted the disk into her computer and opened the file it contained. By the time she'd finished reading the contents it was lunchtime. She made a copy onto her computer. Sealed the original in a jiffy bag and called Hallstone Books to send a courier.

While she was waiting, she made some coffee and a sandwich. She'd need her energy for what she was about to do. The first words on the floppy disk had made her heart beat faster: "If you are reading this it will mean that I am no longer alive. They have won, but I will have the last word."

Hannah leaned back in her chair and stretched. She felt exhausted, but there was also a sense of achievement. The facts were slipping into place. What she couldn't understand was where Edith fitted in. She was convinced that the theft from her studios was a decoy. To distract her from what was really happening. Whoever took those photos must have known there were only copies. It was a delaying tactic. And it had succeeded. In one way. But in another it had revealed the identity of the drowned man. But they couldn't have anticipated that he'd be found so quickly, presumably thinking the body would have been in the water a lot longer.

She looked at her watch. Time to collect Elizabeth.

THERE WAS THE usual mêlée at the nursery. Parents dashing in from their respective work places. Five o'clock seemed to be the rush hour. A lot of teachers, Hannah thought.

"Hi Hannah. What are you doing here?" Hannah looked over at Elizabeth's key worker. "Elizabeth was collected a couple of hours ago."

Hannah could feel the blood draining from her. Fear clutched at her stomach. She thought she was going to throw up. They must be wrong. Of course Elizabeth hadn't been collected. It was a joke. But no one was laughing. She found herself being led to the manager's office and being handed a glass of water.

"Who collected her?"

No one seemed to know. There'd been a changeover of staff. An agency nursery nurse. Everyone was speaking at once. Other parents arrived. Children were collected. Her child was missing. She wanted to scream.

"We'll call all the parents who've already collected and see…"

"No." Hannah had spoken more loudly than she realised and had silenced everyone. "I need to call the police…"

"I really don't think that's necessary. I'm sure it's just a misunderstanding," the nursery manager, Maggie, spoke as though Hannah was an imbecile.

In that moment she could have killed her. Her baby was missing. It wasn't a misunderstanding.

"Maggie, when I first sent Elizabeth here I gave you strict instructions about who could collect her, which you have obviously not followed. I need to call the police."

She took out her mobile phone and dialled Mike Benton's number.

"Mike it's Hannah. Elizabeth is missing."

"What?"

"Someone has collected her from nursery. She isn't here." She felt herself dissolving.

"Stay where you are." He paused. "I'll send out an APB and I'll be with you as soon as I can. Hold it together Hannah."

Faces stared at her. She could feel herself disintegrating. Elizabeth. Please, God, don't let anything happen to her. But it had already happened. The worst possible thing had happened. Someone had taken her daughter.

The manager was still flapping around. Hannah was incandescent. "How could you have let someone else, someone not on my list, take Elizabeth?"

SHE WAS SURPRISED to see lights on in her house as the police car pulled up outside. She didn't want to go inside. Not without Elizabeth. That would somehow make it more real. Janet opened the door and enclosed her in her arms. Gently she led her into the sitting room where she'd drawn the curtains and switched on lamps.

Janet sat next to her on the sofa. Hannah was beyond tears. She was hollow. A shell. Her arms felt the weight of her loss. She couldn't believe this was happening. Elizabeth. The doorbell rang. Janet glanced at the video and went to answer it. Hannah thought she heard loud voices but she was probably imagining them.

She looked at the figure that strode straight over to her and took both her hands in his. "Hannah I'm so, so sorry. We'll do everything we can."

"Rory?" She stared at him. "What are you doing here?"

"DI Benton called me. He thought … Well, Lord Gyles has issued a reward. We're doing everything we can from our end. Just as the police are. You have to stay strong, Hannah."

"I don't understand…"

He looked uncomfortable. "We need a photo of Elizabeth, Hannah and anything you want to say. It will be our front page story tomorrow."

"Tomorrow?" No, tomorrow was too late.

"You need to do this, Hannah." Janet's voice was quiet but firm. There was another ring on the doorbell. Janet disappeared and returned with Claudia Turner.

She nodded at Rory. "I got here as soon as I could."

Hannah was confused. "I'm not working on the case—" Claudia hastily corrected herself. "Elizabeth's abduction. I'm here as your friend."

It was unreal. It couldn't be happening to her, but it was. Her baby had been kidnapped. That word went around and around in her head until she wanted to scream and shout. All this. All these petty intimidations she'd suffered but almost laughed off. It was building up to this. It was her fault. Hers alone. She hadn't taken the hint and backed down and now she was paying the price.

"Excuse me." She made the bathroom just in time to throw up. She retched until she thought her insides were shredded.

Janet was beside her with a glass of water.

"I'm sorry."

"Nothing to be sorry about. Drink some water and wash your face."

Hannah stared at herself in the mirror and didn't recognise the reflection. If anything happened to Elizabeth… She looked at Janet and saw her own grief reflected in her face. She splashed some water on her ravaged visage and when she put the towel to her face she wanted to…

"Are you ready to come downstairs?"

RORY HAD LEFT after a few questions and had taken one of the unframed prints of Elizabeth, which Edith had taken. She'd given her some copies in case she wanted to give them to family. Edith. And she was missing too.

Claudia smiled as she returned. "Mrs Braithwaite sent over some supplies." Hannah vaguely remembered hearing Claudia speaking in the hall when she was upstairs. "Homemade soup and bread. You must eat something or the acid in your stomach will make you feel worse."

Hannah was about to protest, but realised she needed to have her wits about her. She needed to be strong. Janet was fielding any calls to Hannah's mobile. Most seemed to be from journalists from other news groups. Hannah heard a series of no comments.

The soup revived her a little. Her mind raced. "Have they found the agency worker yet?"

Claudia and Janet exchanged a glance. "Not yet. But DI Benton is on the case. He will find Elizabeth for you, Hannah."

"But what if..?"

"Don't torture yourself with what ifs."

She closed her eyes. If only she could sleep and wake to find this had been a horrible nightmare. At some point James arrived. He took her in his arms and hugged her so tightly she could hardly breathe. Janet and Claudia left the room.

"Sorry I must smell awful I came straight from theatre."

"Theatre?" That's where it had all started.

"Operating theatre." He took a couple of phials from his pocket. "I brought you a sedative—just in case."

"No." She looked at him wide-eyed. "I've got to stay awake."

Janet and Claudia came back into the room carrying plates of sandwiches that Leah had also sent over, and a tray of coffee. "You probably need some sustenance too," Claudia said to James. Her smile was encouraging him to lead by example. He obeyed and Hannah nibbled at a sandwich too. It took her forever to chew and swallow the tiniest morsel.

They were all silent.

"Shall we watch the nine o'clock news?"

"Are you sure, Hannah?"

"No, but it's better to know what is being said."

The familiar opening credits of the BBC news faded to Michael Buerk. "We've had breaking news of a kidnapping of a child from a south London nursery." Elizabeth's image filled the screen and Hannah collapsed.

DI BENTON HAD sent a team of uniformed officers to interview every family with a child at the nursery. Not great timing in terms of parents putting their offspring to bed, but maybe it would bring an unguarded comment that would be the break through. He couldn't begin to imagine what Hannah was going through.

He'd had DS Farnham taken into the nick under caution. He was convinced that Farnham was connected in some way. He'd gone through his pocketbook and it was what wasn't there that made him think the DS was involved. Somehow. He'd asked one of the team to check back on all Farnham's arrests, interviews... anything that could link him to Hannah Weybridge. However tenuous. Meanwhile the sergeant could sweat it out in a cell.

So far they'd had no luck finding the agency nursery nurse. Well, they had, but she was in bed ill. Someone had used her ID to impersonate her. This whole affair reeked of careful planning. A sustained and increasingly unpleasant campaign to intimidate Hannah or maybe, through her, Lord Gyles. That was another area of concern. Lord Gyles was never what he seemed. But if he had offended someone, then getting at Hannah—a star in his firmament—would be a good payback.

They had set up an incident room in Dulwich Police Station, a modern building with stables at the rear.

There was a niggle at the back of his mind. The person he really wanted to talk to was Hannah, but would she be in a fit state. He could but try.

THIRTY-NINE

"YOU DID THE right thing coming to me." He handed Fran a crystal glass with a large shot of brandy in it. "But why on earth didn't you come to me before? Am I that much of an ogre?"

She shook her head, sipping the amber liquid, feeling it warm her mouth and throat. She couldn't stop shivering although they were sitting in front of a huge fire and the central heating was also on. She blinked rapidly. Tears would work no miracle she knew. "I'm so sorry. I just…"

"For fuck's sake, don't apologise." Her uncle's hands were clenched so that his knuckles shone white. She knew he would love to punch someone right now but, thank God, it wasn't her.

He came and sat next to her on the sofa. "I'm disappointed you didn't think you could trust me."

"It's not that. I do trust you, but I was just so ashamed."

"Oh, my darling, you have nothing to be ashamed about." His arms tightened around her shoulders. "I will sort this for you. I promise." His finger lifted her chin and she stared into his eyes. Eyes that looked so sad. She had let him down, she knew. "In the meantime, I want you to stay here where you'll be safe."

She nodded. Safety was what she craved.

"I'll have the children collected and brought here."

"Oh, but Phil…"

"Don't you concern yourself about him," he smiled. "Now, I have to make a few calls and I may need to go out. But don't worry, I'll sort it."

She nodded gratefully. The problem had ceased to be hers alone and her uncle had the means to sort it. He touched her cheek tenderly.

"I'll be back soon." His smile was reassuring, but she could sense the tense anger in his body.

ALBERT CROXTON ARRIVED at Fran's house at the same time as two of his men. Albert took the children back to Fran at his house. Phil had been an easy target, but he was just a tiny cog in this pathetic wheel of revenge and an attempt to take over the West End. However, Phil gave them a couple of names, and the owners of those were only too keen to spill more.

Albert Croxton had heard about Sam Smith's death earlier and was furious. He'd put Sam into The Vic as his man. Sadly, that hadn't prevented the tragedy of Joan's death. His beloved friend Joan. For that is what the ex-lovers had become. But he had been well on the way to sorting what needed to be done, when Leo was left for dead and then this happened. Now he would have to work with the authorities. He made another call then left for his meeting.

WITHIN TWO HOURS, the first arrests were made: Roger Priest confessed he had inveigled Joan on to the stage and had spiked her drink. The actor had been told the mixture would only put her out of action for a couple of days. The fool had believed Farnham, who had threatened to release compromising information about the actor—his predilection for young boys—if he didn't do what he was told. Farnham's gambling debts and backhanders from the Downs Mob had finished his career. Life would not be rosy for him in prison.

The DS was singing so loudly he could probably have been heard by his paymasters in their Soho joint, just before an explosion in the men's cloakroom next to the manager's office ricocheted around the building. The place was engulfed in flames within minutes. Firefighters had their work cut out as the smoke and subsidiary explosions impeded their progress.

MEANWHILE, TWO MEN in the Carlton Club finished their drinks and shook hands. One left immediately, while the other made his way to a room he had reserved. It would soon be over, but at what cost? He lit a cigar. And made the last call.

THEY HEARD THE car pull up outside the house. Janet and Claudia metaphorically braced themselves. Imperceptibly, the DCI nodded to Janet. She stood ready. Claudia had the video. The bell rang. She stared hardly believing what she saw. "Answer the door Janet."

And there they were. Her beloved Elizabeth in the arms of Edith who looked hollow eyed and dirty. She almost staggered under the weight of the sleeping child. Janet dragged them both in as the driver made a salute and the car moved off.

Janet took the sleeping child and handed her to Hannah. Silent tears streamed down her face.

"Edith. Oh Edith, what happened to you."

THEY HAD FOUND the woman who had impersonated the nursery nurse. She had been told, she said, it was a custody case and the father needed to see his daughter. This was the only way. She wasn't dumb, but she needed the money and asked no questions. She was glad they hadn't made the connection to Joan Ballantyne. Stupid sods. No one would link her to that. She smirked. The solicitor sitting next to her looked bored and she couldn't blame him.

The door opened and two officers came in and switched on the tape recorder.

"Right I'm DI Benton and this is—" He turned to his colleague "PC Kim Jones."

"Please say your names for the tape."

She looked at the solicitor who introduced himself and nodded to her. "Kath Ryan."

"So, Miss Ryan. Where were you on Sunday the sixteenth of October between the hours of three and six pm."

She stared at him. "I don't understand. I thought I was here about the kid?"

"All in good time." He smiled. For the first time in many hours he could breathe more easily. "We know you visited the apartment of the deceased actress, Joan Ballantyne, on that day."

Her mouth dropped open. "I need a solicitor."

"You have one, here."

"Not him. I need to call my solicitor."

Benson's smile widened. "Now I wonder why that is?"

EDITH HAD BEEN badly shaken by her experience. She'd had a shower at Hannah's, who'd found her some clean clothes and they reheated the soup Leah had brought.

"I went off to what I thought was a commission in Hackney. When I arrived, I was shown in by a young woman—presumably the one who booked me. She took me into a small side room and just locked me in. I can't believe I was so gullible."

Hannah stared at her wide-eyed. "And Elizabeth?"

"She arrived this afternoon. I was so confused by then. But no one harmed her, Hannah."

"Don't worry, we can talk about it all later. But Edith, please forgive me for dragging you into this."

Edith smiled and looked momentarily more like her old self. "No one dragged me, Hannah."

"Who brought you back here, Edith?" Claudia and Janet had been listening. Janet was making notes.

"I think he said his name was Albert can't remember his last name but—"

"Croxton? Albert Croxton?" Janet had supplied the name.

"Could be. He had a child seat in his car. He had come for Elizabeth and was surprised to find me as well."

"Croxton? Is he anything to do with Fran?"

Janet nodded. "Her uncle."

"Oh." Hannah knew it was all piecing together.

THE NEWS RAN a front-page exclusive that spilled over several inside pages about the abduction and return of Elizabeth Weybridge. Hannah wondered where some of the detail had come from, but she drew a blank when she asked Rory.

"Come on Hannah, first rule of journalism—never reveal your sources."

"So you say."

She didn't care. Elizabeth was safe, none the worse for her few hours away from her. And she had been taken to the place where Edith was being held, so she had been there to take care of her.

She needed a few days to be with Elizabeth and then, later, she could write the last chapter of Joan Ballantyne's book.

FORTY

SOME DAYS AFTER the round-up of the people responsible for organising the deaths of Joan Ballantyne and Sam Smith and the abduction of Edith and Elizabeth, Mike Benton had arrived on her doorstep. He hadn't called beforehand and he was alone. Elizabeth was happily playing with her Brio train set, which Hannah had helped her build. Mike squatted beside her.

"How many trains have you got here, Elizabeth?"

Elizabeth, who'd shown no ill effects from her kidnapping, beamed at the DI.

"Three. One, two, three." She pointed to each one.

A young woman walked into the room. "Okay Elizabeth, shall we make some snacks and coffee for mummy and her friend?" She held out her hand, which Elizabeth clasped unhesitatingly, and the pair left the room.

Benton sat opposite Hannah. "She seems nice."

"Yes." Hannah looked away. "I'm not sure I can face nursery again."

The DI studied her face. "Well, give it time." He took a deep breath. "Anyway I'm here to talk about Leo Hawkins."

Hannah felt her face flush. Her scar was demanding attention and her stomach was gripped in an unpleasant spasm. She scratched her hand.

"Yes?"

"He would like to see you."

"I don't understand. Why are you..?" Her eyes filled with tears.

Benton coughed awkwardly.

"When the first responders found Mr Hawkins, he was still just about conscious. He said a few things that didn't seem to make sense, but everything was noted down. He was in a terrible state, Hannah." He paused and stared at his hands. "I saw the photos. I honestly didn't think he'd make it." He shook his head as if to dispel the memory of those images and then smiled. "But he did, Hannah. He did."

Hannah felt a bubble of hope rise.

"In fact, he's doing remarkably well. He was able to help us with the investigation especially about the so-called sister."

Hannah stared at him. "I had heard of the rumours that Joan had been pregnant a second time but there was no mention anywhere of a daughter—or a second son—that I could discover."

The fog in Hannah's mind wasn't clearing. In fact the clouds of coincidence and corruption and suspicion were thickening. Joan seemed to have died for nothing more than petty financial gain and revenge. Disheartening and depressing.

"Yes. A woman phoned Joan Ballantyne's apartment claiming to be her daughter. Leo invited her over, but she arrived with a henchman demanding money which she claimed Joan had arranged to pay her."

"How much?"

Benton was stunned by the question. "Well, I don't suppose it matters if I tell you. Ten thousand pounds."

Hannah's face drained of colour.

"Hannah, are you okay?"

"I have it."

"What?"

"The money. I have it. Leo had it paid into my account by his agent. I only knew after he had been attacked."

Benton waited silently.

"Neville Rogers, my solicitor, advised me to transfer it to a savings account and to wait and see what happened. But I still don't understand. Why did Joan's daughter have her half-brother beaten?"

"It was a scam. The woman purporting to being the daughter was also the so-called nursery nurse who…"

"Excuse me." Hannah rushed from the room and just made it to the bathroom. Benton could hear her retching. He went into the kitchen to fetch a glass of water. The room was empty. No young woman, no Elizabeth. He touched the kettle. Cold. Christ surely this couldn't be happening again? Then he heard their voices coming from the garden and his breathing returned to near normal. He switched on the kettle and returned to the sitting room as he heard Hannah coming down the stairs.

She took the glass he handed her and sipped. With concentration.

"So Joan didn't have another child."

"Not that we know of. And the prints we took from that mug and picture frame you gave us—they matched the woman's. She's the one who'd inverted the photos as well."

Hannah was mystified. "But Joan would have known she hadn't had a daughter so why would she have agreed to pay for her silence?"

"That we may never know, but maybe she was trying to find out who was behind the scam. The woman was being paid to do these things. She confessed, especially when she thought she might be charged as an accessory to murder."

Hannah smiled as the young woman came in with a tray of coffee, placed it on the table and left without saying a word. Then Elizabeth came in, concentrating on carrying a plate. "Biscuits!" She beamed at them.

"Thank you, darling. Offer them to Mike."

Elizabeth did so then said "Bye-bye" and left the room.

"So where does this leave us?"

"Well, everything points to the Downs Mob and their leaders were eliminated in the Soho explosion."

"Which no one has claimed responsibility for."

"Exactly." He had a good idea who the perpetrators were but that wasn't up for discussion now. "We have the minor players and have to be satisfied with that."

Hannah stared into space.

"And poor Joan Ballantyne. All this, all this horror…" the words stuck in her throat. "And Sam dying too."

Sam, she had discovered, had been working for Albert Croxton, who had been warned that someone was trying to get *Lady Heston Regrets* closed down. He guessed it was the Downs Mob, who had invested in another theatre. Sam was there to ferret information about the cast and crew. Obviously not successfully.

Benton was at a loss. Hannah was normally so together. Elizabeth's abduction—however brief—seemed to have sucked the strength from her. She had lost her special sparkle. He wondered idly if Leo Hawkins could reignite it. He hoped so. He liked a happy ending.

FOLLOWING MIKE BENTON'S visit, Hannah made arrangements to visit Leo in hospital. For so long, she hadn't known anything about the state of his health—even if he would survive the assault.

DI Benton, even now, had been evasive, to say the least. She'd contacted his agent, Charles Trafford, who had been equally vague. There had been a news blackout on his condition. Hannah had thought of all the worst-case scenarios. She'd assumed he might not recover, or if he did the injuries he had sustained would be life-changing. Now she could find out for herself.

LEO WAS IN a private ward with a police officer posted on either side of the door. For a moment, Hannah's mind went back to the time she'd come to visit Father Patrick... she pulled her thoughts away and took a deep breath hoping she'd be able to keep her composure whatever Leo looked like.

"Hello Hannah. Thank you for coming."

Hannah had focussed on the bed but the voice came from an armchair near the window. Leo sat with his legs up on a stool. There were shadows on his face—presumably fading bruises—but he looked much better than she'd feared he might.

"Hello Leo. How are you?"

His eyes crinkled. "Probably better than you were feeling when... I'm so sorry I got you into this mess. I had no idea..." He waved at the pile of newspapers he'd kept. *The News* was on top with the story of Elizabeth's abduction and safe return.

"Of course you didn't." She sat down next to him and he clutched her hand.

"Thank you." He looked distraught. "I don't think I've ever been so scared in my life."

Hannah nodded, unsure what to say. In the end, she asked the question uppermost in her mind. "Did you really think your mother had had another child?"

Leo shrugged. "I knew she'd had an illegal termination many years ago. I assumed she wouldn't have made the same mistake twice. I was intrigued as to who this woman was. And I paid the price for my curiosity."

"You certainly did. Although it could have been worse."

"Worse than concussion, a ruptured spleen, emergency surgery and being on a ventilator? Not to mention all the bruises and..."

"Okay, okay." Hannah put her hands up in defeat. "Has anyone else been to see you?"

"Only Charles. He's been amazing."

"You're lucky to have such a good friend. Do you need anything? I suppose that's a stupid question." A glance around the room took in all the get well cards, baskets of fruit… "How do you eat all that?"

"I don't. I pass them on to the children's ward or wherever. The nurses are appreciative." He just about managed a wink. "Shame really."

"Good thing I came empty handed then."

"But you came, Hannah. And your inquiries helped discover what had happened to my mother. I am so grateful. Thank you."

EPILOGUE

THE LILLIAN BAYLIS Bar was heaving. Hannah surveyed the scene and was reminded of the last time she had been here: Joan Ballantyne's wake. Quite a few of the same people had been invited, with some obvious exceptions.

"Nervous?"

She turned to see Sir David Powys standing by her side. He handed her a glass of champagne.

She smiled, remembering her first impressions of the director when he had seemed unnecessarily offensive to her. "I am. I'm not used to being in the spotlight."

His expression was thoughtful. "No, I don't suppose you are. Don't worry. Speak slowly. Smile. Rob said you did it perfectly when he did the run-through with you."

Hannah had been amazed at the thought and planning that had gone into the launch. Being coached by the theatre's sound engineer was the least of it. Obviously this was a major production for everyone concerned.

"Is your photographer friend here?"

A smile played about her lips. "Edith? Yes she is." In her peripheral vision she caught sight of Georgina talking to now DCI Claudia Turner. Mike and Phoebe Benton were here too, as well as Janet. All as guests. Such a fruit salad mixture of a guest list. Neville Rogers chatting to Linda and David. Yvonne was too near her due date to attend. Celia and Mary chatted with Diana and James.

"You look amazing by the way. This is your show. Remember that." He smiled, and turned to talk to someone who claimed his attention.

Lord Gyles approached with Albert Croxton. His niece, Fran, had been booked for the catering and was looking super-efficient with her team of waiters.

"Hannah, we're going to start in a few minutes." Lord Gyles looked satisfied with the turnout of book reviewers and celebrity writers, not to mention a few TV personalities. He smiled encouragingly and glanced over at the table piled high with copies of the book she would be expected to sign. Someone claimed his attention and he moved away.

Albert Croxton touched her arm.

"Thank you for booking Fran for this. It was a lovely gesture. Just the confidence boost she needed."

Memories of… "I was happy to recommend her, Mr Croxton."

He raised an eyebrow. "I'm sure you can manage Albert, Hannah."

Fortunately, she didn't have to reply as Rory appeared at her side. "Excuse me Hannah, there's something we need to check." He gently pushed her into the crowd.

"What is it?"

"Nothing."

"Nothing?"

He sighed. "You looked like a rabbit caught in headlights. Don't let that man get under your skin. Just because…"

Just because he'd rescued Edith and Elizabeth. But Hannah did feel intimidated. Caught. She didn't want to be beholden to him. Although, to be fair, he'd never implied she was. So much had happened. So many people implicated. A cesspit of corruption.

"Ladies and gentleman." The room hushed as Lord Gyles spoke from the small dais that had been erected. "Thank you all for coming to the launch of this exciting book. Well, the lead up to it getting published certainly had its moments." Polite titters. "Just a couple of months ago, we lost one of our most accomplished actresses, Joan Ballantyne, who had been working on her memoir with one of my most distinguished journalists at *The News*. So why would Hannah Weybridge, known for her intrepid investigations be working with an actress? It was supposed to keep her out of harm's way and allow her to recover from an assault on her life. Maybe it was prescience, serendipity or what you will that she was around to ask the questions about Joan's death and to pursue her quarry? She paid a price. Again. But I am delighted to introduce you to her this evening as the co-author of *Joan Ballantyne: A Life*. Please welcome… Hannah Weybridge."

Hannah stepped up beside Lord Gyles, who led the applause and then left her alone on the dais. There was a strong smell of Chanel No 5. It felt like a benediction.

"Thank you." She paused and smiled.

Direct your comments to someone in the audience, she had been told. Her eyes found Jessica Jewel and she smiled.

"I thought this commission would be a metaphorical walk in the park. How wrong can you be? I hope I have done justice to Joan's life and career. I'd like to thank all her friends and colleagues, who gave their time so generously to me, so that the book could be finished. In spite of all their help, I struggled, because I didn't know how or why Joan died. We know that now." For a moment her voice sank into a hoarse whisper then rallied. "Much of this book is Joan in her own words and those of you who knew her will recognise her wit, and her sometimes forensic criticisms."

Hannah looked up. At the back of the room she could just make out a wheelchair negotiating the crowd. Gradually a pathway opened up and the wheelchair approached the dais. Immediately it was surrounded. And when the cloud of people dispersed, Hannah saw him. Supported on crutches, making his painful way to join her, was Leo Hawkins. His face was a picture of concentration, determination. She felt as though the whole room was holding its collective breath. Their eyes met and a smile illuminated his face. Hannah knew she had to hold it together, but it was so hard.

"Ladies and gentlemen, as you can see, our guest of honour has arrived to steal my limelight, for which I am truly grateful." She moved to one side. Leo's presence seemed to stun the guests. Hannah hadn't known until an hour before that he would be joining them.

Now, he balanced precariously beside her and spoke eloquently of his mother and her achievements and praised Hannah's work on the book. The rise and fall of his voice calmed Hannah, but his words were lost to her as, across the room, she saw Lord Gyles and Albert Croxton standing together again. Why hadn't she noticed the similarity between these two powerful men before? What was their connection? Both men looked straight at her. The hairs on the back of her neck tingled. They had ensnared her in their web and she needed to know why. She would be free of them but now was not the moment.

"...and for that I have Hannah Weybridge to thank. I hope you all enjoy *Joan Ballantyne: A Life.*"

Leo leaned forward and kissed her amid a battery of camera flashes and resounding applause. She made her way to the signing table with Leo following slowing behind her. This evening she would enjoy the party, but she would keep Lord Gyles and Albert Croxton in her sights. Tomorrow, or the day after, or next week, the real work would begin.

ACKNOWLEDGEMENTS

I began writing *Stage Call* during the first lockdown in 2020. At the time I had started a contemporary psychological thriller but found it difficult to concentrate. An idea for another Hannah Weybridge came to me and I found refuge back in the 1990s.

The pandemic has scuppered so many plans and projects not least in publishing. I have been so fortunate that when my publisher, Urbane Publications, ceased trading in March 2021, Sean Coleman of Red Dog Press was interested in adopting Hannah Weybridge. Sean and his team produced new editions—including hardbacks— of the first four books in the series with exquisite new covers and a text refresh in preparation for the publication of *Stage Call*.

Writing books set in the 90s throws up odd research questions at times. As usual I am so fortunate in having friends in various fields who help me with facts. None more so than Dr Geoff Lockwood my medical advisor who not only checks facts and offers suggestions but always makes sure they are appropriate to the time. He hasn't yet taken me up on the offer to write medical thrillers together.

My contact in the Met remains anonymous for professional reasons but was able to confirm details of the CBI with colleagues who were active in 1994. Thank you.

There are two other names checks. When I was being interviewed for UK Crime Book Club, one of the admin said she'd love to be a named character in a book: enter Caroline Maston as a theatrical agent and thank you for sharing some personal details that I've included and adapted.

Take-away curries feature heavily in the Hannah Weybridge series and in my life during lockdown! My post launch party dinner for *Perdition's Child* was held at Dulwich Tandoori and since then they have been amazing supporters of my books especially Nurul who reads all the blog posts and reviews and agreed to be named in this book (although he wouldn't have been old enough to work there then!).

As always, my thanks to my wonderful family and friends who support me with their love and encouragement and especially to Katherine Lyon and Tim Clark who've taken to hosting dinner parties to celebrate my launches.

Most of all my gratitude goes to the book community—authors, bloggers, reviewers and readers who have taken Hannah Weybridge to their hearts. Thank you for your support, which means so much and is hugely appreciated.

And lastly this book is dedicated to my mother, Joan, whose father's name was Ballantyne. She taught me to read and instilled a love of books, theatre and film. She read voraciously, from the poetry of Andrew Marvel to Charles Dickens with Catherine Cookson as one of her all-time favourites. She also read everything I wrote including my translation of an erotic novel but sadly didn't live to see the publication of my crime novels. I hope she would have enjoyed them and would have loved the nods to members of our family whose idiosyncrasies have lived on in my characters.

ABOUT THE AUTHOR

For most of her working life in publishing, Anne has had a foot in both camps as a writer and an editor, moving from book publishing to magazines and then freelancing in both.

Having edited both fiction and narrative non-fiction, Anne has also had short stories published in a variety of magazines including *Bella* and *Candis* and is the author of seven non-fiction books.

Telling stories is Anne's first love and nearly all her short fiction as well as *Dancers in The Wind* and *Death's Silent Judgement* began with a real event followed by a 'what if ...'; That is also the case with the two prize-winning 99Fiction.net stories: *Codewords* and *Eternal Love*. *Stage Call* is her fifth thriller starring investigative journalist Hannah Weybridge.